Remarkable Women: Past and Present

The Literary Crowd

Remarkable Women: Past and Present

The Literary Crowd

Writers, Critics, Scholars, Wits

Kitty Benedict and Karen Covington

A Harcourt Company
Austin • New York
www.steck-vaughn.com

Published by Raintree Steck-Vaughn Publishers, an imprint of
Steck-Vaughn Company

CREATED IN ASSOCIATION WITH MEDIA PROJECTS INCORPORATED
C. Carter Smith, *Executive Editor*
Carter Smith III, *Managing Editor*
Kitty Benedict and Karen Covington, *Principal Writers*
Ana Deboo, *Project Editor*
Bernard Schleifer, *Art Director*
John Kern, *Cover Design*
Karen Covington, *Production Editor*

RAINTREE STECK-VAUGHN PUBLISHERS STAFF
Walter Kossmann, *Publishing Director*
Kathy DeVico, *Editor*
Richard Dooley, *Design Project Manager*

Photos on front cover, clockwise from top left: Judy Blume,
Fanny Burney, Rita Dove, Virginia Woolf

Photos on title page, top to bottom: Willa Cather, Zora Neale Hurston,
Selma Lagerlöf, Marguerite Yourcenar

Library of Congress Cataloging-in-Publication Data
Benedict, Kitty.
The literary crowd: writers, critics, scholars, wits / [compiled by] Kitty Benedict and Karen Covington.
p. cm. — (Remarkable women: past and present)
Includes index.
Summary: Brief biographies of 150 women who have made significant contributions to literature and criticism, from poet Virginia Hamilton Adair to novelist and scholar Maria de Zayas y Sotomayor.
ISBN 0-8172-5732-2
1. Literature—Women authors—Biography—Juvenile literature. 2. Women authors—Biography—Juvenile literature. 3. Women critics—Biography—Juvenile literature. 4. Women journalists—Biography—Juvenile literature. 5. Litterateurs—Biography—Juvenile literature. [1. Authors. 2. Critics. 3. Women—Biography.]
I. Covington, Karen. II. Title.
PN471.B46 2000
809'.89287—dc21 98-54938
[B] CIP AC
Printed and bound in the United States
1 2 3 4 5 6 7 8 9 0 LB 03 02 01 00 99

CONTENTS

INTRODUCTION

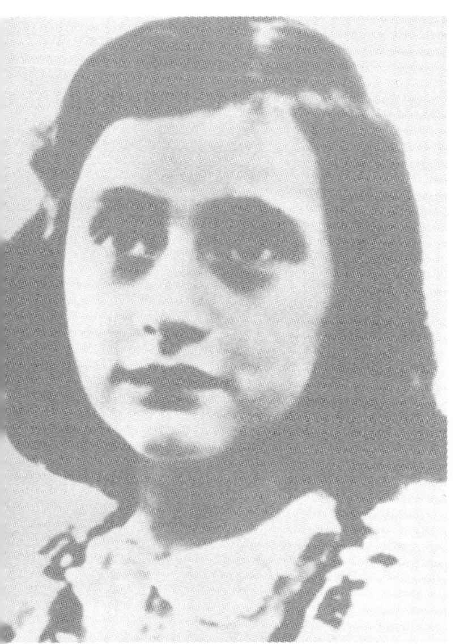

How is it possible to choose just 150 women writers for such a book as this? The answer is, simply, that it can't be done. Or, of course, it *can* be done, but more people have had to be left out than could be included, and among those omitted are many beloved writers.

Isn't it encouraging, though, that there are so many brilliant women writers—far, far too many to fit in the cramped space between the covers of this one limited book? Throughout history women who might have been wonderful writers have been denied education or the opportunity to exercise their talents. But so many made their way nonetheless! Over 1,000 years ago in Japan, the budding writer Murasaki Shikibu eavesdropped on her brother's Chinese lessons to learn a language she would otherwise never have known. Fifty years ago in Amsterdam, Anne Frank, denied her freedom by the Nazis who eventually murdered her, managed to record her thoughts so beautifully that her diary has been read by millions.

Any woman who *is* included in this book is certainly worth reading. We have deliberately chosen women who write in all different styles, who come from all different places and times. There are the most famous of the famous, like Jane Austen, Emily Dickinson, and Virginia Woolf. There are people you have probably never heard of, such as Julian of Norwich, Ding Ling, and Ama Ata Aidoo. There are novelists, poets, short-story writers, historians, essayists, critics, letter writers, and women who did all or most of those things.

Reading is time travel and world travel. Sappho's poetry will transport you to ancient Greece. Harriet Beecher Stowe's *Uncle*

Tom's Cabin will teach you about slavery before the Civil War. Ursula Le Guin's books will take you into the future. Books can also show you how much you have in common with their authors. Love, jealousy, fear, and anger haven't changed much over time. It can be thrilling to learn, for example, that in the 11th century in Japan, the opinionated Sei Shonagon could not "bear people who, without really understanding the subject, join in a conversation . . . and who confuse the issue with their irrelevant remarks."

Another great thing about reading is that your tastes grow as you do. Maybe this year the idea of reading Barbara Tuchman's *The Guns of August* or Harper Lee's *To Kill a Mockingbird* or Gertrude Stein's *Tender Buttons* doesn't sound appealing. One day you just might find yourself wondering how World War I started. Or maybe you'll wonder what it was like in the segregated South of the 1950s. Or perhaps you might want to puzzle over Stein's eccentric love of language.

So read. Read about the women in this book, and explore what they did and wrote. Browse the shelves at the library, the bookstore, and at friends' houses. Keep an open mind, and remember that if you have questions, some of the wisest women in the world might have thought about the same things. If you want to enjoy an adventurous tale, many dashing women have written one. If you want to lose yourself in beautiful language, collect interesting words as if they were butterflies, and contemplate gorgeous imagery, women poets have written those things down. You have a lot of good reading ahead of you.

Photos top left Anne Frank, bottom left Edna St. Vincent Millay, top right Lorraine Vivian Hansberry, bottom right Harper Lee.

Virginia Hamilton Adair (1913–)
Poet

POETRY HAS PLAYED A ROLE IN VIRGINIA ADAIR'S life from the beginning—she can remember sitting in her crib listening to her father read out loud to her from the *Iliad*. She began writing poetry at age six. Leaving her girlhood home in New Jersey, she attended Mount Holyoke College in Massachusetts, where she won several prestigious awards.

After marrying historian Douglass Adair in 1937, Virginia busied herself raising their three children and sometimes taught college literature courses. As always, she wrote poetry. Occasionally she published pieces in such magazines as *The Atlantic Monthly*, but she had little interest in actively promoting her work. In 1955 the Adairs settled in Claremont, California, where she has remained ever since, teaching and writing.

In 1968 Douglass suddenly committed suicide, leaving no explanation. The poetry Virginia wrote in the years after that tragedy expresses the anguish and confusion she felt. Finally, when she was 83 years old, a fellow poet, Robert Mezey, convinced her to publish her work and helped her to select and arrange poems for the collection *Ants on the Melon* (1996). It received both critical and popular praise. Her second volume, *Beliefs and Blasphemies: A Collection of Poems*, followed in 1998. Adair is blind as a result of glaucoma, but she continues to write using an old manual typewriter.

Ama Ata Aidoo (1942–)
Poet, playwright, novelist, short-story writer

THE DAUGHTER OF AN AFRICAN CHIEF, AMA ATA Aidoo grew up in a royal household in central Ghana. She was given a western-style education, graduating from the University of Ghana with an honors degree in English. She studied at Stanford University in California and has taught at universities in Ghana, Kenya, and America. Aidoo has also served as Ghana's education minister.

Aidoo wrote her first play, *The Dilemma of a Ghost*, at age 22, while she was still in college. In it, a young Ghanaian man returns home after studying abroad, bringing with him an American wife. Neither of them are aware of how hard it will be to live in the African community. Aidoo does not believe western ways are better than African ways, only that it is not easy to combine them. Many of her later works come back to this idea.

Aidoo often writes about the exploitation of women and slaves in a materialistic, nonspiritual world. Her language is a blend of traditional African spoken narratives—folktales, gossip, children's stories—and western literary forms. Her books include a second play, *Anowa* (1970), the novel *Changes: A Love Story* (1991), and *The Eagle and the Chickens* (1986), a collection of children's stories.

Anna Akhmatova (1889–1966)
Poet

BORN IN THE UKRAINE IN THE COASTAL CITY OF Odessa, Anna Gorenko began writing as a young girl. She took her grandmother's surname, Akhmatova, as a pseudonym when she published her first book of poetry, *Evening*, in 1912.

At the beginning of her career, Akhmatova and her husband, Nikolai Gumilev, helped to start a new poetic movement known as Acmeism. The Acmeists valued clarity and truthfulness, in contrast to the obscure language in the Symbolist poetry that was fashionable at the time. Akhmatova's early poems were lyrical expressions of love. But her most famous poetry was written during the persecutions that followed the Russian Revolution. Her work expressed her passion for her home country and a craving for freedom, love, and life.

Akhmatova refused to flee the country, although, like many intellectuals of the time, she suffered persecution and loss. Gumilev was executed, her son was imprisoned, and many of her writer friends were killed or committed suicide. Akhmatova herself was condemned by the Communist party and prevented from publishing for years. Her long cycle of poems, "Requiem," was smuggled out of Russia and printed in Paris in 1963. After Stalin's death the government gradually eased the censorship it had inflicted on Akhmatova. In 1964 she was permitted to travel abroad, where she was honored for her work. At her funeral, thousands of Russians came to show their love for this great poet and woman of dignity.

Louisa May Alcott (1832–1888)

Novelist, essayist, suffragist

Louisa May Alcott is one of America's most beloved writers. Her novel *Little Women*, which has been a best-seller since it first appeared, is based on Alcott's own family life in Massachusetts.

As a girl, Alcott was a tomboy, not unlike Jo in *Little Women*. In spite of her independence, however, a spirit of self-sacrifice ruled her life. Her father, Bronson Alcott, an idealist and prominent Transcendentalist, did not believe in working for wages, and the family was terribly poor. By the age of 16, she supported her parents and three sisters single-handedly, mostly by writing short stories for magazines under an assumed name.

During the Civil War, Alcott worked briefly as a nurse in Washington, D.C., until she contracted typhoid fever. The book that she published about her experience, *Hospital Sketches* (1863), earned her critical praise. Even so, money remained her reason for writing. She produced many sensational tales of passion, murder, and madness. Over a century after her death, these works attracted the attention of feminists and scholars, who brought them back into print. *Behind a Mask* (1975) is a collection of Gothic stories that she wrote during this time. Then in 1868, at her publisher's suggestion, Alcott began writing a story for girls. The success of *Little Women* and its six sequels ended Alcott's financial worries forever.

A feminist, Alcott wrote essays in the 1870s supporting women's suffrage and was the first woman to register to vote in Concord, Massachusetts. She continued to put duty to her family first. Although her own health was poor, she cared for her father and niece until her death at age 56, only two days after that of her father.

Claribel Alegría (1924–)

Poet, novelist, essayist

Claribel Alegría was born in Nicaragua, but because her father was sympathetic to the Sandinista rebels, the family was forced to flee the country when she was six months old. They moved to El Salvador, where she remained until she went to the United States to go to college in 1943.

As a student at George Washington University, in Washington, D.C., Alegría began writing poetry. She also met her husband, the journalist Darwin Flakoll, who would later collaborate with her on many projects. She published poetry, short fiction, and children's stories, and until 1959, when the Cuban Revolution occurred, her focus as a writer was mostly personal.

Since the revolution, she has made her political beliefs an integral part of her art. In her essays and her fiction, she speaks out against the cruel dictatorships in Central America, particularly in her two homelands, Nicaragua and El Salvador. Her works include the bilingual collection of poetry *Flores del volcán/Flowers from the Volcano* (1982) and the novel *Cenizas de Izalco* (1966, Ashes of Izalco), which she wrote with Flakoll. In addition to their home in Nicaragua, the couple also keep a house in Spain.

Isabel Allende (1942–)

Novelist, journalist, feminist

By 1973 Isabel Allende had over a decade's experience as a journalist and a television personality in Santiago, Chile. Her successful career came to a sudden halt, though, when the military dictator, Augusto Pinochet, seized power. Salvador Allende, Chile's first democratically elected president—and Isabel's uncle—was assassinated. It was soon too dangerous for her to remain. Allende fled to Venezuela with her husband and two children.

When she found out that her grandfather, still living in Chile, was dying, Allende began a letter to him, incorporating her memories and the stories he used to tell her. The letter evolved into her first novel, *La casa de los espíritus* (1982, The house of the spirits), a family saga that blended myth, fantasy, and reality. This style is often called "magic realism." Her three subsequent novels, *De amor y de sombra* (1987, Of love and shadows), *Eva Luna* (1988), and *El plan infinito* (1993, The infinite plan), share that quality. Romantic yet politically charged, they were all best-sellers.

Paula (1995), a reflection on her family, politics, and feminism, also began as a last letter to a loved one, this time her fatally ill daughter. The act of storytelling and remembering helped her to bear her grief. Currently, Allende lives in San Francisco with her second husband.

Maya Angelou (1928–)

Poet, autobiographer, actress, dancer, teacher

Maya Angelou, born Marguerite Johnson, has told the story of her varied and colorful life in six volumes of autobiography, beginning with *I Know Why the Caged Bird Sings* (1970), an instant best-seller. Each succeeding volume found a wide audience, and the most recent, *Wouldn't Take Nothing for My Journey Now,* was published in 1993.

Born in St. Louis, Missouri, Angelou was three years old when she and her brother went to live in Arkansas with their grandmother. "Momma" Henderson exercised great influence on the little girl, particularly after Angelou was abused at age eight by a family friend while visiting her mother. She stopped speaking for five years, but Momma never lost confidence in Maya, telling her she would one day bring her message to the world as a preacher.

Angelou has published several volumes of poetry, and was commissioned to write a poem for the inauguration of President Clinton in 1991. In "On the Pulse of the Morning" she asks Americans to live up to their democratic ideals and to celebrate the beauties of life. Reading it at the ceremony, Angelou felt her grandmother's prophecy had been fulfilled.

Angelou's life experience is vast and varied. She has been a waitress, a dancer, an actress, a playwright, a screenwriter, the first black woman streetcar conductor in San Francisco, a teacher, and a civil rights activist. She has experienced abandonment, homelessness, drug abuse, and discrimination. But, as she says in a poem: "You may trod me in the very dirt/ But still, like dust, I'll rise."

> **"She said that I must always be intolerant of ignorance but understanding of illiteracy. That some people, unable to go to school, were more educated and even more intelligent than college professors. She encouraged me to listen carefully to what country people called mother wit. That in those homely sayings was couched the collective wisdom of generations."**
>
> **Maya Angelou**
> ***I Know Why the Caged Bird Sings***

Hannah Arendt (1906–1975)

Philosopher, political theorist

Born into a Jewish family in Hanover, Germany, Hannah Arendt learned to read before she was five. At university she studied with the famous philosophers Martin Heidegger, Edmund Husserl, and Karl Jaspers. When Hitler came to power in 1933, Arendt emigrated to Paris. She was forced to flee again in 1941, after the Germans occupied France. Arriving in New York City with her mother and husband, she began to write essays on politics, racism, and nationalism for intellectual magazines like *Partisan Review* and *The Nation.*

Her first book, *The Origins of Totalitarianism*, was published in 1951, shortly after she became an American citizen. Examining the history of anti-Semitism, Arendt attributed the rise of totalitarianism in Western Europe to the development of mass society. Alienated from each other and their communities, she argued, people no longer shared a moral system and became vulnerable to dictatorships. Another major and controversial work was *Eichman in Jerusalem: A Report on the Banality of Evil* (1964), her account of the infamous Nazi war criminal's trial.

Arendt continued to produce influential books and articles. She taught at American universities, including the University of Chicago and the New School for Social Research, and she was the first woman to be made full professor at Princeton University. Brilliant, original, and controversial, Hannah Arendt was a major figure in 20th-century political theory.

Aspasia of Miletus (5th century B.C.E.)

Intellectual, literary figure

ASPASIA, BORN IN MILETUS IN THE PROVINCE of Anatolia, was a famous courtesan, or *hetaera*. Extraordinarily beautiful and intelligent, she was just as well educated as a man. Since she was a foreigner living in Athens, Aspasia was free from the social customs that restricted Greek women, so she often held the company of politicians, artists, and philosophers. The city's most important intellectuals gathered at her house to discuss their ideas and learn from one another—not least from Aspasia herself. Plato said she taught him the theory of love. Socrates delighted in her brilliance.

Pericles, the leader of Athens, fell in love with Aspasia. The two lived together for over 15 years until his death in 429 B.C.E. She supported his attempts to establish a democratic government and helped to write his speeches. Political opponents frequently attacked her for her private life and influence over Pericles. At one point, she was accused of atheism and brought before the High Court. But Pericles made a passionate speech in her defense, and the jury acquitted her.

Margaret Atwood (1939–)

Poet, novelist, critic

MARGARET ATWOOD HAD AN UNUSUAL childhood. Her father was an entomologist who studied bees, caterpillars, and spruce budworms. So, from the age of six months, she spent part of every year in the wilderness of northern Ontario and Quebec, where her father did his fieldwork. Atwood did not go to a regular school until she was 12, but she began writing poems, plays, and stories when she was five years old.

In 1961, the year Atwood graduated from the University of Toronto, her first collection of poems, *Double Persephone*, was published. The book received several awards. She went on to graduate school at Radcliffe and Harvard. Although she accepted teaching positions at Canadian universities, she concentrated mostly on her writing and by 1972 was able to pursue it full-time.

Remarkably prolific, Atwood has published over 30 books, ranging from collections of poetry to literary criticism to children's books (for which she also provided the illustrations). Atwood is active in feminist causes, and her political beliefs and Canadian heritage are important elements of her work. Her novels include *The Edible Woman* (1969), *The Handmaid's Tale* (1986), and *Alias Grace* (1996).

Jane Austen (1775–1817)

Novelist

WOMEN LIKE JANE AUSTEN, LIVING AT THE turn of the 19th century, were strictly limited in their opportunities. Marriage was almost the only way they could survive economically. With that goal in mind, they were expected to be genteel and modest, experts in the feminine arts of music and needlework. Austen had all these skills in abundance, and it is likely that she received several proposals, but neither she nor her dear sister, Cassandra, ever married.

As a girl growing up in Hampshire, England, Austen read as much as she could and wrote stories and plays to entertain her family. Even though her father valued education and encouraged hers, nobody took her "scribbling" all that seriously. Jane herself was so modest that she published her novels anonymously. However, she was well aware of her abilities, and determined to succeed.

Although historic events such as the Industrial Revolution and the Napoleonic Wars attracted many of her contemporaries, Austen concentrated on what she knew best: the daily events of English village life. Exploring human nature with a keen eye, she described the dance of courtship necessary in the pursuit of a proper marriage. Her heroines are smart, funny, and independent, but they usually mature and go through a process of moral education before the story ends.

"She had not been brought up . . . to know to how many idle assertions and impudent falsehoods the excess of vanity will lead. Her own family were plain matter-of-fact people, who seldom aimed at wit of any kind; her father at the utmost being contented with a pun, and her mother with a proverb; they were not in the habit, therefore, of telling lies to increase their importance, or of asserting at one moment what they would contradict the next."

JANE AUSTEN
Northanger Abbey, **1818**

In 1817 Austen became sick, probably from cancer. She died in Cassandra's arms at the age of 41. Her work had been well received even during her lifetime. Today her novels, which include *Pride and Prejudice* (1813) and *Emma* (1815), are considered among the best in English literature.

Djuna Barnes (1902–1982)

Novelist, playwright, poet

DJUNA BARNES, BORN IN Cornwall, New York, was educated by her artist father at home. She studied art in New York City, but soon turned to journalism to earn a living and support her mother and brothers. Her articles appeared in the *Brooklyn Eagle*, *New Republic*, and the *New Yorker*, among other national publications.

In 1919 and 1920, three of Barnes's plays were staged by the Provincetown Players, and for most of the 1920s, Barnes lived in Paris, socializing with expatriate writers such as James Joyce and Gertrude Stein. The brooding novel, *Nightwood* (1936), is her masterpiece, an exploration of the dark, subconscious parts of the mind. Her willingness to describe extreme behavior and her detached, nearly comic, view of violence shocked many readers. But T. S. Eliot praised her writing for its "beauty of phrasing" and its "quality of doom and horror."

At the end of her life, Barnes lived in New York's Greenwich Village, refusing to see anyone. Her work remains of interest for its penetration into the deep recesses of the human heart. Perhaps even more significant is her fame as a literary personality in New York and Paris during the 1920s and 1930s, when she was friends with many of the most important writers and artists of her day.

Sylvia Beach (1887–1962)

Publisher, bookseller

IN 1919 SYLVIA BEACH OPENED SHAKESPEARE AND Company, a combination of American bookstore, lending library, and general gathering place for literary expatriates in Paris. The shop was a home away from home, where Beach provided comfort, encouragement, and unwavering devotion to the writers she called "pilgrims of the twenties."

Born in Baltimore, Maryland, Beach got her first taste of Paris life when she was 14 and her father, a Presbyterian minister, was sent to serve at the American Church there. She returned in 1917 to study, and after she opened Shakespeare and Company, Paris became her permanent home.

The shop attracted such writers as Ernest Hemingway, Ezra Pound, and Gertrude Stein. Beach made a direct contribution to modern literature when she published James Joyce's *Ulysses* (1922), which had been censored in England and America. Passionately dedicated, she single-handedly forced the novel into print and continued her association with Joyce long after, although he often took advantage of her willingness to work for him.

When the Nazis occupied France during World War II, Beach was forced to close the shop, and she later spent several months in an internment camp. But she returned as soon as she could, remaining in Paris until her death at age 75.

Simone de Beauvoir (1908–1986)

Philosopher, novelist, essayist, critic

IN *THE SECOND SEX* (1949), SIMONE DE BEAUVOIR discusses the history of western women, arguing that in patriarchal societies, a woman is defined almost solely in terms of biology, as the object on which the male projects his desires and demands. "She sees herself and makes her choices not in accordance with her true nature, but as man defines her," Beauvoir wrote. Shocked anger and ridicule greeted the book, which was condemned by the Vatican as anti-Catholic. However, it was immediately popular among women; 20,000 copies were sold in the first two weeks after its publication in France. It has influenced feminist literary, historical, and psychological thinking for decades.

Beauvoir was born into a middle-class Parisian family, whose ideals she quickly rejected. Reading Louisa May Alcott and George Eliot inspired her to become a writer. She studied philosophy at the Sorbonne, where she met Jean-Paul Sartre, who would be her companion for life, intellectually and emotionally. The ideas they developed together were to become central to the philosophical movement known as Existentialism.

Beauvoir wrote four volumes of fascinating autobiography, five novels, and essays on politics, current affairs, and philosophy. An influential critic of French and American societies, Beauvoir protested against social injustice throughout her life, and in 1974, signed a manifesto supporting a woman's right to abortion. In one of her last books, *The Coming of Age* (1970), she attacked growing discrimination against the elderly.

Aphra Behn (1640–1689)

Dramatist, novelist, poet

KNOWN AS THE FIRST ENGLISHWOMAN TO MAKE A living as a professional writer, Aphra Behn's origins are obscure. Scholars have debated whether her maiden name was Amis Johnson, but it is known that a girl named Aphra (or Aphara) lived in Suriname in South America in the first half of the 17th century.

About 1658, she married a Dutchman named Behn, who took her back to England and then died, leaving her impoverished. Aphra approached King Charles II for help and was commissioned to travel to Holland as a spy. This she did, but the government never acknowledged her reports. She returned to London desperately poor and was sent to debtors' prison. After her release, she started to write: poetry, plays, novels, translations, and prose. Her literary output was huge.

Behn's most famous work, the romantic novel, *Oroonoko: Or, The History of the Royal Slave* (1688), tells the story of a slave rebellion she witnessed in Suriname. Like other novels she wrote, it presents a woman fighting for her independence.

Behn was outspoken about the sexual double standards of her time and wrote bawdy comic plays, which were greatly popular with actors and audiences. She was a lively personality and inspired many scandalous rumors. In spite of the celebrity she achieved during her lifetime, the circumstances of her death, like those of her birth, are obscure.

Gwendolyn Bennett (1902–1981)

Poet, graphic artist, short-story writer, educator, journalist, editor

A CHILD OF DIVORCED PARENTS, GWENDOLYN Bennett was kidnapped by her father when she was eight years old and did not meet her mother again until she was 22. Nevertheless, she had a stable upbringing with her adored father. The pair lived in several places, then settled in Brooklyn, New York. At high school there, Bennett wrote poetry and won prizes for her artwork. Undeterred by restrictions on blacks, she enrolled in the art program at Columbia University in 1921. She also went to Pratt Institute, Howard University, and spent a year in Paris.

Bennett came of age during the Harlem Renaissance, and she was an active participant, along with Langston Hughes, Zora Neale Hurston, and W. E. B. Du Bois. She was an exuberant poet and artist, and a vibrant personality. "It was fun to be alive and to be part of all of this . . . you always had an exciting time," she recalled later. Bennett wrote for many journals, including the NAACP's *Crisis*. Her column "The Ebony Flute," followed the cultural doings of the African American community.

During the 1930s, Bennett turned to arts administration. She was head of the Harlem Community Arts Center from 1938 to 1941. Gradually retiring from public life, she spent her later years in Pennsylvania with her second husband.

Elizabeth Bishop (1911–1979)

Poet

EIGHT MONTHS OLD WHEN HER FATHER DIED, Elizabeth Bishop was only five when her mother was hospitalized in a mental asylum. So, at an early age she became a nomad, living with her mother's relatives in Nova Scotia, then returning to her home state, Massachusetts, to her father's family. While at Vassar College, Bishop met the poet Marianne Moore, who became one of her best friends and encouraged her to become a writer.

Always, Bishop traveled as much as possible. She went to Newfoundland, Europe, and North Africa before settling briefly in Key West, Florida, and then Mexico. During a trip to South America in 1951, an allergic reaction forced her to stop in Brazil, where she stayed for 18 years with a wealthy Brazilian woman, Lota de Macedo Soares. Many of the poems in her collection *Questions of Travel* (1965) are about this time. Toward the end of her life, she returned to Massachusetts to teach at Harvard University.

Geography and the allure of travel figure prominently in Bishop's work. She is a writer of refined sensibility, a celebrator of beauty. Although the body of her work is slight—she published only four books—Bishop ranks among the best 20th-century American poets. She received many awards, including the Pulitzer Prize for a book containing her first two volumes of poetry, *North & South* and *Cold Spring* (1955).

Judy Blume (1938–)

Novelist

JUDY BLUME'S PHENOMENAL SUCCESS COMES FROM her ability to describe the fears and feelings of young people. Growing up in New Jersey in an Orthodox Jewish family, Blume felt unable to express her important feelings to her parents. They seemed unaware of her adolescent torments. Blume married during her junior year at New York University and had two children after graduation. Disturbed by nagging illnesses, she looked for creative outlets. Doing housework, Blume started making up children's stories, then returned to NYU to study writing.

Her first book, *The One in the Middle Is the Green Kangaroo*, was published in 1969. With her third book, *Are You There, God? It's Me, Margaret* (1970), she discovered her voice—a funny, conversational monologue by a central character, whether age 10 or 30. Blume has since published more than 20 novels, including *Blubber* (1974) and *Tiger Eyes* (1981) for younger readers, as well as *Wifey* (1978) and *Summer Sisters* (1998) for adults. Her controversial subjects—divorce, sexuality, pregnancy—drew such a response from young readers that she published *Letters to Judy: What Your Kids Wish They Could Tell You* (1986), to encourage parents to communicate with their children.

Nellie Bly (1867–1922)

Investigative journalist

"NELLIE BLY" IS MOST FAMOUS FOR THE AROUND-the-world trip she completed in 1890 while working for Joseph Pulitzer's *New York World*. By boat, train, and ricksha, she challenged the fictional journey made by Phileas Fogg in a popular novel, *Around the World in Eighty Days*. Americans eagerly followed her progress through England, France (where she met Fogg's creator, Jules Verne), Egypt, Singapore (where she bought a monkey), China, Japan, San Francisco, and New York City. The whole journey took her 72 days, 6 hours, and 10 minutes—and made her an international celebrity.

More significantly, Bly was an ingenious investigative reporter who fought her way into the almost exclusively male domain of news reporting. She risked life and limb to bring back stories of injustice, usually by unscrupulous business and political leaders. She wrote about women factory workers, slum dwellers, and peasants in Mexico. Once she posed as a patient to reveal barbarous conditions at a mental asylum on Blackwell's Island in New York City. As a crusader she had few peers.

Born into a genteel family in Pennsylvania, her true name was Elizabeth Cochran. In 1885, angered by a Pittsburgh newspaper article claiming that "girls" were only good for domestic work, she wrote such an impressive letter to the editor of the Pittsburgh paper that he hired her, assuming she was a man. At first she sent in articles signed "E. Cochrane," but after revealing her true identity, she adopted her famous pseudonym.

Two years later, Bly marched into the offices of the *New York World*, demanded an assignment, and got it. She married in 1895, but returned to journalism after her husband's death. Her obituary called her "the best reporter in America."

Louise Bogan (1897–1970)

Poet, critic

Louise Bogan was born in Maine into an Irish-American family. They lived in several New England mill towns before settling in Boston, where Bogan finished high school and attended a year of college.

Bogan's life was scattered with difficulties. An early marriage lasted only two years. Living in New York, she worked to support her daughter and at the same time wrote poetry for magazines. Her first collection, *Body of This Death* (1923), received critical praise. After remarrying in 1925, she moved to a farm and wrote *Dark Summer* (1929). That peaceful time ended when the house burned down, destroying her papers. Bogan went on to become poetry critic for the *New Yorker* and traveled in Europe on a Guggenheim fellowship in 1933. She returned to a crumbling marriage but, as always, refused to surrender to depression. Although she produced less poetry as time passed, she wrote criticism, memoirs, and many letters to her friends.

Bogan's highly disciplined lyrics often take on a dreamlike quality as they explore spiritual and psychological questions. She always strove to create beauty out of her struggles with despair.

Kay Boyle (1903–1992)

Novelist, short-story writer, poet

Although she was born in Minnesota, Kay Boyle spent most of her childhood in Europe and the eastern United States. She attended college in Ohio briefly, then moved to New York City, where she worked for the experimental literary magazine *Broom*. She was friends with many writers of the day, in particular the poet William Carlos Williams.

Boyle's three marriages—to a Frenchman, an expatriate American, and an Austrian refugee—kept her mostly in Europe between 1923 and 1953. There she witnessed firsthand the events leading up to World War II and incorporated her experiences into her writings.

Boyle published poetry and short fiction in magazines throughout her career. Her first novel, *Plagued by the Nightingale*, appeared in 1931. Perhaps most appreciated as a short-story writer, she won the O. Henry Prize twice, for "White Horses of Vienna" (1935) and "Defeat" (1941). After 1963, she taught at San Francisco State University. Always politically active, she was a member of the Anti-Vietnam War movement in the late 1960s.

Anne Bradstreet (1612–1672)

Poet

Anne Dudley was born in Northampton, England, and educated privately in the elaborate surroundings of Tattershall Castle, where her father was steward. At age 16, she married Simon Bradstreet. Two years later, when her father was appointed deputy governor of the Massachusetts Bay Colony, the family set sail for New England.

Bradstreet's first book appeared in London without her knowledge. Her brother-in-law collected poems she sent home to her relatives and published them as *The Tenth Muse Lately Sprung Up in America* (1650). However, it is her second book that is most appreciated today. *Several Poems Compiled with Great Variety of Wit and Learning* (1678) was published after her death and contains revisions of her early poems as well as later pieces. It is the work of an accomplished poet. Bradstreet examined nature, spirituality, and human emotion with the eye of a romantic as well as a Puritan. Many of the poems reflect her deep love for her husband and eight children.

Anne Bradstreet lived for 42 years in the Massachusetts Bay Colony, where her husband eventually became governor. She is the first colonist known to have published poetry.

"I am obnoxious to each carping tongue
Who says my hand a needle better fits,
A Poet's pen all scorn I should thus wrong,
For such despite they cast on Female wits:
If what I do prove well, it won't advance,
They'll say it's stolen, or else it was by chance."

Anne Bradstreet
Prologue to *Several Poems Compiled with Great Variety of Wit and Learning*

Anne, Emily, and Charlotte Brontë

Charlotte Brontë (1816–1855)
Emily Brontë (1818–1848)
Anne Brontë (1820–1849)

Novelists

CHARLOTTE, EMILY, AND ANNE BRONTË BECAME novelists under unlikely conditions. Living at Haworth Parsonage on the lonely English moors, they saw few people other than their stern father and the aunt who raised them after their mother died. Their lives were isolated and streaked with tragedy. But they nourished their talents and fueled their imaginations by writing and storytelling.

After their two oldest sisters died of tuberculosis at boarding school, Charlotte and Emily, who were also at the school, returned home to be educated. One day, their brother, Branwell, received a gift of toy soldiers, and each of the four children adopted one. Over several years, they made up mythical homelands for their soldiers: the kingdoms of Gondal and Angria, complete with history, politics, legend, and other characters.

As young women, Emily and Charlotte were teachers for a time, and Anne was a governess. Unhappy in these jobs, they reunited at Haworth, determined to support themselves as writers. In 1846 Charlotte published a collection of their poems under the pseudonyms of Currer, Ellis, and Acton Bell.

Emily's novel *Wuthering Heights* and Anne's *Agnes Grey* were both accepted by a publisher, but did not appear until after an editor rushed Charlotte's *Jane Eyre* into print in 1847. *Jane Eyre* was a success, but the other two were not, and when it was learned that the Bells were women, critics were outraged. Their writings, especially Emily's, were termed "coarse," "implausible," and "unfeminine."

Then tragedy struck the family again. Branwell died in 1848, addicted to alcohol and opium. Within a few months, Emily and Anne died of tuberculosis. Charlotte published two more books before marrying the Reverend Arthur Bell Nicholls in 1854. She was working on a novel when she suffered complications from pregnancy and died.

Today Charlotte and Emily's books are classics. *Jane Eyre* is perhaps the best known, the story of a governess and her love for the brooding Mr. Rochester. *Wuthering Heights* is a passionate tale of conflict and love between Catherine Earnshaw and Heathcliff. Anne's work is also worthy of attention, especially her second novel, *The Tenant of Wildfell Hall* (1848).

Gwendolyn Brooks (1917–)

Poet

GWENDOLYN BROOKS WAS A BABY WHEN HER family moved from Topeka, Kansas, to the South Side of Chicago, and she has lived there ever since. She has made the lives of the black residents in that community the subject of her powerful and meticulously crafted verse.

Brooks's mother always encouraged her to write. The two went to poetry readings together, where they met the authors James Weldon Johnson and Langston Hughes. She was still a teenager when her first poems were published. After graduating from Wilson Junior College, Brooks was invited to take part in a poetry workshop taught by the socialite and intellectual Inez Cunningham Stark.

Brooks published her first volume of poems, *A Street in Bronzeville*, in 1945. Her next book, *Annie Allen* (1950), was the first work by an African American to receive the Pulitzer Prize. Her early poems are known for their sensitive portrayal of the black urban experience, especially of the lives of women. In the 1950s, she began to address questions of racial injustice, and at a writers' conference in 1967, she met members of the black arts movement who inspired her to express her political ideas more emphatically. Leaving her long-time publisher, Harper & Row, she began to work exclusively with small African American presses.

A Distinguished Professor of English at Chicago State University and the Poet Laureate of Illinois, Brooks has received many awards for her work. She has been married to Henry Blakely since 1939.

Elizabeth Barrett Browning (1806–1861)

Poet

Elizabeth Barrett was a prodigy, writing her first poem when she was four years old, an epic poem at 14, and a philosophical poem at 16. She became famous for her poetry and translations from Greek. In 1844 the poet Robert Browning wrote her a fan letter, begging to meet her. She did not grant his request at first. At the time she was living in London with her family. She was a reclusive invalid dependent on morphine to dull the physical pain of her chronic illness and the grief she had suffered since her beloved brother's death four years before.

Elizabeth and Robert began by corresponding. Then they met, and friendship became passionate love. Against her father's will, Elizabeth secretly married Robert Browning in September 1846 and escaped with him to Italy. Disinherited by her father, she never saw him again. Later he returned all the letters she sent to him from Italy, unopened.

The Brownings took up residence in Florence, and she gave birth to a son in 1849. She published the 44 "Sonnets from the Portuguese" she had written during her courtship and the narrative poem "Aurora Leigh" (1856). Both poets became involved in the Italian independence movement, and she fervently expressed her political sympathies in her last works. Although she was happier than she had ever been, Elizabeth's health declined again, and in 1861 she died in her husband's arms.

Pearl Sydenstricker Buck (1892–1973)

Novelist, humanitarian

Just three months after her birth in West Virginia, Pearl Buck was brought to China by her missionary parents. She learned to speak Chinese before English and developed a lifelong devotion to the country. Among her many projects

were the East and West Association to promote intercultural understanding and the Pearl S. Buck Foundation to help half-American children in Asia. An outspoken opponent of racism, she protested the internment of Japanese Americans during World War II.

From 1917 to 1934, Pearl was married to John Buck, an agricultural specialist living in China. When they divorced, she married her publisher, Richard Walsh, and settled in America. In addition to a daughter from her first marriage, Buck adopted eight children from varying racial backgrounds. Always in search of money to support her family and her humanitarian causes, she published as much as possible, sometimes up to five books a year. Her lifetime literary output was, therefore, prodigious: over 100 books, plus articles, speeches, and plays. *The Good Earth* (1931), her most famous novel, is about the peasants of Anhwei province. It won a Pulitzer Prize and was translated into 30 languages. In 1938 Buck became the first American woman to receive a Nobel Prize for Literature.

Julia de Burgos (1914–1953)

Poet, journalist

Julia de Burgos grew up outside San Juan, Puerto Rico, near the banks of the Río Grande de Loíza, a river that often appeared in her writings. Her large family had little money, but supportive neighbors helped pay for her schooling. She graduated from high school with honors and earned a teaching certificate from the University of Puerto Rico in 1933. A passionate supporter of Puerto Rican independence and an advocate of social change, she went on to teach in a rural village and to produce educational radio programs. Her first book of poetry, *Poemas exactos a mí misma* (1937, Exact poems to myself), brought her to the attention of the local literary crowd. Her next volume, *Cancíon a la verdad sencilla* (1939, Song to simple truth), received national recognition with the Institute of Puerto Rican Literature award.

After 1940 Burgos lived mostly in New York City. She was acclaimed for her work as a journalist and married the writer Armando Marín. But she suffered increasingly severe depression. She died suddenly from complications related to alcoholism, and for several days her body was unidentified. When her husband discovered what had happened, he arranged for the burial she had requested, by the Loíza River. She remains a beloved public figure, both for her poetry and the example she set as a social activist and feminist.

> **"I wanted to be like men wanted me to be:**
> **an attempt at life;**
> **a game of hide and seek with my being.**
> **But I was made of nows,**
> **and my feet level upon the promissory earth**
> **would not accept walking backwards,**
> **and went forward, forward,**
> **mocking the ashes to reach the kiss**
> **of the new paths."**
>
> **Julia de Burgos**
> **"I Was My Own Route"**

Frances Hodgson Burnett (1849–1924)

Author, children's writer

Frances Hodgson's life changed drastically after 1854, the year her father died, leaving his family with little means to survive. In search of a better existence, they moved from England to America in 1865. They settled in Tennessee, expecting an uncle to help them, but he did not, so Frances was forced at an early age to earn a living.

In 1868 she sold her first story, and within a few years was contributing regularly to magazines. She published her first novel, *That Lass o' Lowrie's*, in 1877, not long after her marriage to Dr. Swan Burnett. Always popular, she received her widest recognition yet, with her first book for children, *Little Lord Fauntleroy* (1886). Burnett's children's books, especially *A Little Princess* (1905) and *The Secret Garden* (1910), are still widely read and adored.

A recurrent theme in her stories, maybe because of her own early experience, is the child faced with going from rags to riches, or riches to rags. Her villains treat children badly just because they are poor, but Burnett shows that, regardless of appearances, it is the person inside who counts.

Fanny Burney (1752–1840)

Novelist, letter writer, diarist

THE ENGLISH WRITER FANNY BURNEY PUBLISHED her social satire, *Evelina: Or, The History of a Young Lady's Entrance into the World* in 1778. In it, she told the comic story of a young woman learning—by trial and error—the manners that she needed to succeed in society.

The daughter of the musician Charles Burney, Fanny had been a shy child. But once her identity as the author of *Evelina* was revealed, she met many distinguished literary figures and impressed them with her wit. Burney's diaries from this era provide entertaining accounts of scenes she witnessed and conversations she had with her famous contemporaries. In 1782 she published her second successful novel, *Cecilia: Or, Memoirs of an Heiress.*

After spending a few years at the court of Queen Charlotte and King George III, Burney married Alexandre d'Arblay. The couple lived in near poverty, and she was forced to write so that they had enough money to survive. None of these later works brought the success of the earlier novels. Fanny Burney died at the age of 87. Afterward, her diaries and letters were published to great acclaim.

Angela Olive Carter (1940–1992)

Novelist, short-story writer, journalist

SHORTLY BEFORE SHE WAS DIAGNOSED WITH cancer, the British writer Angela Carter had insured her life for an immense amount of money. Characteristically, she took a perverse joy in knowing that her husband and son would soon inherit a fortune. Carter's writing can be described as Gothic horror, science fiction, adventure, magic realism, surrealism, and fairy tale. All those elements are woven through her highly colored prose, often couched in wildly comic terms.

Carter's father was a journalist, a path she also followed before earning a degree in literature at Bristol University in 1965 and turning to fiction. Her travels, particularly to Japan, fired her imagination, as did the work of such writers as Edgar Allan Poe and Jorge Luis Borges.

Admired for her short stories as well as for her novels, Carter's books include *The Magic Toyshop* (1967), *Nights at the Circus* (1984), and the story collection *Burning Your Boats* (1996). She was 51 years old when she died.

Willa Cather (1873–1947)

Novelist, editor, critic

BORN IN VIRGINIA, WILLA CATHER MOVED TO Nebraska with her family when she was ten. At first the harsh prairie land frightened her, but soon she developed a deep love for it. At school, Cather studied Greek and Latin, acted in amateur plays, and mystified the townspeople when she took to dressing like a man, cropping her hair, and calling herself William Cather, M.D.; she could never stand to be a submissive female.

Cather graduated from the University of Nebraska with a strong interest in literature, art, and music. She edited a women's magazine and taught English and Latin for ten years in Pittsburgh, where she lived with Isabelle McClung, her lifelong companion. A frequent contributor to national publications, Cather took a job in New York as staff writer for *McClure's* magazine in 1906 and published her first novel, *Alexander's Bridge*, in 1912. Among the popular novels that followed are *O Pioneers!* (1913), *My Antonia* (1918), *A Lost Lady* (1923), and *Death Comes for the Archbishop* (1927).

Although Cather's books have always been appreciated by the public, they went out of favor with critics after her death. Recently, however, her

writing has been reassessed. She is now recognized as an extraordinary stylist who reveals complex emotional states, and explores essential themes and conflicts of life on the American frontier.

Kate Chopin (1851–1904)

Novelist, short-story writer

BORN IN ST. LOUIS TO AN IRISH FATHER AND AN aristocratic Creole mother, Kate O'Flaherty was a respectable young lady with a streak of proud independence. She wrote and smoked Turkish cigarettes, in rebellion against the conformity required of society belles. At age 19, she married a cotton broker named Oscar Chopin and moved to New Orleans.

Widowed in 1882, Chopin returned to St. Louis and began writing again. Rejecting the sentimental style of American Victorian fiction, she modeled her work on French authors such as Gustave Flaubert and Guy de Maupassant. Her first published novel, *At Fault*, appeared in 1890. She also wrote over 100 short stories, collected in *Bayou Folk* (1894) and *A Night in Acadie* (1897). Critics proclaimed them charming. Actually, her finely drawn tales pulsed with undercurrents of protest against marriage, racism, and the Victorian womanly ideal.

In *The Awakening* (1899), however, the subversive nature of Chopin's writing became clear. The story of a woman who chooses love and independence over life, it describes female sexuality in beautiful language. The shocked outcry of readers could be heard across the country. Chopin was accused of trying to corrupt American morals, her last book of short stories was left unpublished, and she essentially stopped writing. It was not until the 1960s that her skill at portraying the interior world of women was rediscovered and *The Awakening* was recognized as her masterpiece.

Agatha Mary Clarissa Christie (1890–1976)

Mystery writer, playwright

IN 1971 AGATHA CHRISTIE WAS KNIGHTED DAME Commander of the British Empire. She considered having tea with Queen Elizabeth II after the ceremony one of the high points of her life. The author of more than 80 novels, plays, and short-story collections, this "Duchess of Death" has enthralled millions with the exploits of her detectives, Hercule Poirot and Miss Jane Marple.

Agatha Christie (right) views a likeness of herself at Madame Tussaud's Wax Museum in London.

Christie's father was American, her mother English. She was raised in Torquay on the southwest coast of England. Imaginative and dreamy as a child, she wrote her first story while in bed with the flu when she was 18. She married the flying ace Archie Christie at the age of 24 and, while he was at war, worked in a hospital dispensary, collecting knowledge of poisons. Her second husband, Max Mallowan, was an archaeologist. He once worried that she might not enjoy his profession digging up bodies, but she exclaimed, "I *adore* corpses and stiffs!"

Christie's books are strictly plotted, witty, and—although she reveals all clues—scattered with false leads. Among her most famous mysteries are *Murder on the Orient Express* (1934), and *Death on the Nile* (1937). Her play, *The Mousetrap*, (1952) ran in London for over 45 years.

Beverly Cleary (1916–)

Children's author

FOR NEARLY 50 YEARS, BEVERLY CLEARY'S POPULAR books for young people have entertained children and parents alike. Set in a middle-class neighborhood in Portland, Oregon, the stories are

> **"There were two kinds of children who went to kindergarten—those who lined up beside the door before school, as they were supposed to, and those who ran around the playground and scrambled to get into line when they saw Miss Binney approaching. Ramona ran around the playground."**
>
> BEVERLY CLEARY
> *Ramona the Pest*

about ordinary boys and girls. They are remarkable for their good humor and for their sensitivity to the secret shames and anxieties of childhood. They also acknowledge the delight children take in mischief-making, silliness, and cleverness.

Raised in Oregon, Cleary discovered the excitement of reading at age six, but remembers being disappointed that so many of the children's books she read were not entertaining or had nothing to do with the world she knew.

After graduating from the University of California at Berkeley, she became a children's librarian. She married and, in 1950, began to write about Henry Huggins and his dog, Ribsy. Her most beloved character, Ramona Quimby, appeared in the *Henry Huggins* books, and with the publication of *Ramona the Pest* in 1968, she graduated to a series of her own. In 1983 Cleary published *Dear Mr. Henshaw*, dealing with the topic of divorce. Cleary has written over 40 books and has received numerous national and regional awards.

Colette (1873–1954)

Novelist

THE SPICE AND VARIETY OF COLETTE'S LIFE evoked both warm admiration and shocked disapproval from those who followed her career. When she died at the age of 81, the French government honored her with a lavish state funeral, but the Catholic Church denied her a religious burial service because of her celebrated exploits.

She was born Sidonie-Gabrielle Colette in Burgundy, France. In 1893 she married Henri

Gauthier-Villars, who routinely published other writers' articles under his pen name, "Willy." He proceeded to pass off his wife's first four novels—about a heroine named Claudine—as his own.

Determined not to continue being exploited, Colette obtained a divorce in 1906 and began performing in Paris music halls. This scandalized everyone she knew, but it was a way for her to assure her independence. Her experiences in the theater also inspired an extremely successful novel, *La vagabonde* (1910, The vagabond).

While continuing to publish fiction, Colette worked as a newspaper editor and critic, and even operated a beauty school for a time. Her marriage to Henri de Jouvenel, the editor of the newspaper *Le Matin* (The Morning), resulted in the birth of a daughter. In 1925 she fell in love with writer Maurice Goudeket; they married a decade later. Goudeket, who was Jewish, was imprisoned during World War II, causing Colette considerable anguish.

Colette's writing is notable for its bittersweet humor and vivid evocations of details as subtle as odors, tastes, and sounds. Among her many novels are *Chéri* (1920) and *La fin de Chéri* (1926, The last of Chéri), *La chatte* (1933, The cat), and a fictionalized reminiscence named after her beloved mother, *Sido* (1929). The recipient of numerous awards, she was named a Grand Officer of the Legion of Honor in 1953.

Anna Comnena (1083–1153)
Historian

ANNA COMNENA WAS THE OLDEST CHILD OF Alexius I, ruler of the vast Byzantine Empire. Like her mother, Irene Dukas, and her grandmother, Anna Dalassena, Comnena was strong-minded and intelligent. Her knowledge of Greek classics, astronomy, geography, and political affairs was extensive.

Comnena never reconciled herself to the fact that her brother would inherit the throne even though he was five years younger than she was. With her mother's support, she attempted repeatedly—and unsuccessfully—to seize power for her husband, Nicephorus Bryennius. So, when her brother was crowned Emperor John II in 1118, she was forced to leave the court. Eventually, she withdrew to a convent and wrote an account of her father's reign, becoming the first-known female historian.

The *Alexiad* provides inside information about court happenings, important personages, military exploits, and international relations. Comnena was especially contemptuous of western Crusaders who seemed to be interested only in violence and looting the capital, Constantinople (modern-day Istanbul), of its treasures.

Elena Cornaro-Piscopia (1646–1684)
Philosopher

BORN IN VENICE, A MEMBER OF THE ITALIAN nobility, Elena Cornaro-Piscopia was the first woman to receive a doctorate in philosophy. Famed for her learning as a girl, Elena knew seven languages and studied mathematics, religion, and music. She went to the university at Padua simply to study. Her father encouraged her to seek a formal degree—and persuaded the reluctant university to award it to her.

Elena's doctoral examination in 1678 attracted many spectators, who were awed by her brilliance. However, her achievement was so remarkable for its time that it was almost as if she were a performer rather than a scholar. There was little she could do with her degree, since it was unacceptable for a woman to teach at the university. She chose not to marry but devoted herself to study and charitable works until her death at age 38. Her poems and speeches were published four years later.

Shelagh Delaney (1939–)
Playwright

SHELAGH DELANEY'S FIRST PLAY, *A TASTE OF Honey*, was produced in 1958 by the Theatre Workshop in London. With its humorous and sensitive look at British working-class characters, the play distinguished itself at a time when theater was almost all written by and for the middle class. Critics uniformly praised the play. A few, however, believed it owed its success to Joan Littlewood, the director and producer. After all, they argued, the 19-year-old playwright had never finished school.

Raised in the industrial town of Salford in Lancashire, England, Delaney enjoyed grammar school, but by the age of 16 was tired of studying and ready to start earning a living. Working at a succession of odd jobs, she also began writing a novel. One night she came home from seeing a play convinced that she could do better. She adapted the story line of her novel for the stage and sent the manuscript to the Theatre Workshop. Two weeks later, *A Taste of Honey* went into production.

The play ran in London for several years, was successfully produced in New York in 1960, and was made into a film in 1962. Although her next play, *The Lion in Love* (1962), did not do well critically, Delaney has been a successful writer for television and film.

Anita Desai (1937–)

Novelist, short-story writer

KNOWN FOR HER MYSTERIOUS, GOTHIC WRITING style, Anita Desai is one of today's most celebrated Indian authors. She received recognition with her very first novel, *Cry, the Peacock*, in 1963 and has gone on to publish novels, short stories, and works for children.

Desai was raised in Delhi by her Indian father and German mother. She attended private English-speaking schools, but spoke German to her family and Hindi to friends. After graduating from the University of Delhi in 1957, she moved to Calcutta, where she met and married Ashwin Desai. The couple has since lived all over India; she has also held teaching fellowships in England and the United States.

Many Indian writers, Desai among them, have been criticized for writing in English—a colonial language—rather than a native one such as Hindi. But Desai is specifically interested in examining modern Indian society, in which many languages are spoken. She is widely praised for her in-depth look at complex and sometimes dark characters. Emily Brontë's *Wuthering Heights* was one of her early influences. Desai's novels *Clear Light of Day* (1980) and *In Custody* (1984) were nominated for the British Booker Prize.

Emily Dickinson (1830–1886)

Poet

EMILY DICKINSON, ONE OF THE GREATEST American poets, published only seven poems in her lifetime. After her death, her sister, Lavinia, found a wooden box filled with small booklets containing over 1,700 handwritten poems, and in 1890 they were published.

Her life seems simple: The daughter of a dominating father, Dickinson rarely left the village of Amherst, Massachusetts. She attended Mount Holyoke College for a year. Beneath the quiet surface, however, a subversive intelligence flourished. As a young girl she was popular, witty, and appealing, but her best friends were her books. She steadily withdrew from the outside world as she matured. Some scholars suggest that she chose isolation rather than resisting a rigid patriarchal society. Dickinson played the piano, took walks with her dog, baked, and gardened. She wrote many letters to friends she rarely or never saw in person. She was close to her sister and to Susan Gilbert, her sister-in-law. And all the time, she jotted lines of verse on scraps of newspaper, worked them over, then copied them out.

"The brain is wider than the sky,
For, put them side by side,
The one the other will include
With ease, and you beside.

The brain is deeper than the sea,
For, hold them, blue to blue,
The one the other will absorb,
As sponges, buckets do.

The brain is just the weight of God,
For, lift them, pound for pound,
And they will differ, if they do,
As syllable from sound."

untitled poem, EMILY DICKINSON

In her poetry, Dickinson pursued the large truths contained in ordinary events—"Tell all the Truth/But tell it slant." Starting with familiar hymn-like rhythms, Dickinson loved to depart into the unexpected by using eccentric words, varied tempos, and broken rhymes. She could be sly or whimsical, and she could be irreverent, even outrageous.

Along with Walt Whitman, Emily Dickinson transformed 19th-century American poetry. Her legacy has been a powerful inspiration to writers ever since.

Joan Didion (1934–)

Novelist, essayist, journalist, screenwriter

JOAN DIDION'S CAREER AS a writer began just after her graduation from the University of California at Berkeley in 1956. As the winner of *Vogue*'s Prix de Paris writing competition, she was awarded a job at the magazine's offices, so she moved to New York City.

It didn't take long for other magazines to begin publishing Didion's work. In 1963 her first novel, *Run River*, appeared. In the book, Didion reflects upon the myth of the great American West, which saturated her childhood in the Sacramento Valley. The following year Didion married John Gregory Dunne and returned to California. Settling in Los Angeles, the couple collaborated on screenplays. Didion continued to publish on her own, producing such works as her collection of essays, *Slouching Toward Bethlehem* (1968), and the novel *Play It as It Lays* (1970).

Didion has received praise for her eloquent prose and realistic portrayal of late 20th-century society. In her controversial essays, she has examined topics ranging from the hippie culture of the 1960s to the depression she has experienced in her personal life. Her work provides readers with thought-provoking commentary and observations, reflecting many of the concerns of the day.

Ding Ling (1904–1986)

Short-story writer, essayist

CHIANG WEI-CHIH—BETTER KNOWN BY HER pseudonym, Ding Ling—established her career as a short-story writer in Peking during the 1920s. With their unique view of the inner lives of modern young Chinese women, her stories attracted a strong following. The most famous of them is "The Diary of Miss Sophie" (1928).

Ding Ling was in love with a poet, Hu Yeh-p'in, whose involvement with the Communist party made him a target of the Nationalist government. The pair moved to Shanghai, hoping to escape persecution, but he was executed in 1931. From then on, she dedicated her writing to the Communist cause and was even imprisoned for her outspokenness.

In 1949 the Communists came to power, but Ding Ling's political troubles were not over. She was rejected by the party in 1958 because she could not accept all their ideals unquestioningly. Most controversially, she believed in the artist's individual creativity and that women should have social equality. For the next 21 years, Ding Ling was nearly erased from Chinese cultural memory. Her work was burned, and she was exiled to a faraway province.

Freed in 1975 and eventually readmitted to the Communist party, Ding Ling resumed her career, publishing essays and short stories until her death.

Assia Djebar (1936–)

Novelist, filmmaker

BORN IN ALGERIA WHILE THE COUNTRY WAS STILL a French colony, Assia Djebar became involved with the liberation movement in the late 1950s. Her writings reflect her political involvement. The anti-colonial novel, *La soif* (1957, published in English as *The Mischief*), was written during the student revolts of 1956, and *Les enfants du nouveau monde* (Children of a new world) was published in 1962, the year Algeria became a democracy.

The role of women in society and in the struggle for liberation was a central theme in Djebar's early work. After the war, she focused on Algeria's growing feminist movement. And in the late 1970s, while teaching at the University of Algiers, she became a filmmaker.

Djebar wanted her message to reach as many people—particularly women—as possible. Because of illiteracy among the people, books were not the best way. The characters in her films speak an Arabic dialect that most Algerians understand. Using her voice as both a writer and filmmaker, Assia Djebar has become one of the most influential women artists in her country.

Hilda Doolittle (H.D.) (1886–1961)

Poet, novelist, memoirist

BORN IN BETHLEHEM, PENNSYLVANIA, H.D. WAS strongly influenced by her upbringing in the Moravian religion, a German Protestant sect. Her elusive poems require careful decoding; they are filled with meaningful imagery, especially from classical mythology, which fascinated her.

At age 15, Doolittle met the 16-year-old poet Ezra Pound, who remained a lifelong influence on her. Together they studied Latin, Greek, classical myth, and poetic technique. Doolittle started at Bryn Mawr College but left in 1906, after having a breakdown, possibly because of her turbulent relationship with Pound, to whom she had become engaged.

In 1911 Doolittle moved to London to be near Pound. There she became part of a large literary circle that included D. H. Lawrence, T. S. Eliot, Amy Lowell, and her future husband, the poet Richard Aldington. She also began to write poetry, helping to define the style known as "Imagism." During this time, she adopted the pseudonym H.D.

From her first collection, *Sea Garden* (1916), H. D. was recognized as an innovative writer. She often examined her difficult personal life in her work. During World War I, her brother and her father died, and she divorced Aldington. She struggled with depression and was seriously ill when she gave birth to her daughter. Friendship with the wealthy Winifred Ellerman (known as "Bryher") brought her much comfort. Among her most famous works are the Imagist-era *Collected Poems of H.D.* (1925) and her long poem, "Helen in Egypt" (1961).

Rita Dove (1952–)

Poet, short-story writer, novelist

RITA DOVE GREW UP IN AKRON, OHIO, IN A middle-class family where learning was highly respected. In a house filled with books, the children were encouraged to read whatever interested them. After graduating *summa cum laude* (with high honors) from Miami University in Ohio, she went to Germany on a Fulbright Fellowship. There she was fascinated by the sensation of being an outside observer in an unfamiliar culture, an idea she has since explored in her poetry.

In her intricately crafted poems, Dove often examines personal issues within the larger framework of culture or history. The historically based poems in *Museum* (1983) reveal "the politics behind the artifacts, the stories behind the legends." In the Pulitzer Prize–winning *Thomas and Beulah* (1986), the poems collectively provide a portrait of a couple modeled on her grandparents. Just as Dove provides in-depth portraits of others, she has also used poetry

to examine the facets of her own identity as woman, African American, mother, wife, and daughter. The Poet Laureate of the United States from 1993 to 1995, Dove is currently a professor at the University of Virginia.

Ariel Durant (1898–1981)

Historian

AN AMBITIOUS, TALENTED WOMAN IN HER OWN right, Ariel Durant is forever associated with her husband's work. She contributed to all 11 volumes in their series, *The Story of Civilization*, but did not receive coauthor's credit until the seventh book.

Ida Kaufman was a toddler when her Jewish parents emigrated from Russia to New York City. As a high school student, she fell in love with one of her teachers, and he gave her the pet name—Ariel—which she later adopted legally. She was 15 when she roller-skated to City Hall to marry 29-year-old Will Durant.

Ariel steadily established herself in New York's intellectual circles. She cofounded the Gypsy Tavern, a popular artists' hangout, and gave a lecture series, "Women of the Great Salons," which was later adapted for the *Story of Civilization*. From their start of the history project in 1930, Ariel organized Will's notes. Increasingly, she contributed information and helped to plan the books. *The Los Angeles Times* named her a woman of the year in 1965, and the Durants won a Pulitzer Prize in 1967.

The couple remained together to the very end. Ariel and Will Durant died within two weeks of each other in Los Angeles, their home after 1943.

Marguerite Duras (1914–1996)

Novelist, script writer, filmmaker, journalist

MARGUERITE DURAS'S LITERARY CAREER SPANNED 53 years and included novels, plays, screenplays, and short stories. In her tales, passionate love, often touched by violence, occurs against a richly colored background. Her distinctively fragmented yet simple language casts a hypnotic mood, conveying events as if through the characters' own consciousness.

Born Marguerite Donnadieu, she lived for her first 18 years in French Indochina (present-day Vietnam), where her parents were teachers for the French colonial service. She changed her name when she was in her 20s. Her experiences there provided the setting for many of her novels, particularly *Un barrage contre le Pacifique* (1952, The sea wall) and *L'amant* (1984, The lover). The latter sold more than two million copies, was awarded the Prix Goncourt (a major French literary prize), and became a successful movie.

During World War II, Duras joined the French Resistance and the Communist party. Expelled from the party in 1950, along with other intellectuals, she became disillusioned with ideological groups, although her work retained a political element. Her masterful script for the film *Hiroshima mon amour* (1959) brings together the desecration of atomic war and desperate longings for love and fulfillment. In addition to writing, she worked as a television journalist and a filmmaker.

George Eliot (1819–1880)

Novelist

GEORGE ELIOT WAS ONE OF THE FIRST ENGLISH novelists to use her art to examine the human heart and mind as well as to entertain. In contrast to the plot-driven, sensational stories of her day, Eliot's novels delve into the psychological and sociological forces at work on her characters. Events progress in a way that is believable, insightful, and effective.

Born Mary Ann Evans, she was a serious student and was at first drawn to Evangelical Christianity. Later, her philosophical studies led her to renounce organized religion, although her sense of right and wrong remained firm. Moving to London in 1849, she became an editor at the *Westminster Review*. There, she fell in love with the critic George Henry Lewes. Although estranged from his wife, Lewes could not get a divorce, so the couple lived together without marrying, in shocking defiance of Victorian social custom. Mary Ann also began to write fiction, using the pseudonym George Eliot so her work would not be prejudged as "feminine."

In her major novels, which include *Silas Marner* (1861), *Middlemarch* (1871), and *Daniel Deronda*

"If we had a keen vision and feeling of all ordinary human life, it would be like hearing the grass grow and the squirrel's heart beat, and we should die of that roar which lies on the other side of silence."

GEORGE ELIOT
Middlemarch

(1876), Eliot dissects the ways people react to social pressures, often straying from the path they know is right. Many authors have acknowledged the impact of her achievement. Charles Dickens admired her realism and lack of melodrama, and Virginia Woolf called *Middlemarch* "one of the few English novels written for adult people."

Enheduanna (approximately 2300 B.C.E.)

Poet, high priestess

ENHEDUANNA WAS THE DAUGHTER OF POWERFUL Sargon the Great, the Akkadian king who conquered the ancient Sumerian city of Ur. After his victory, Sargon made his daughter the high priestess of the Sumerian moon god, Nanna. Archaeologists have found a number of texts, mostly hymns, that bear Enheduanna's seal and in which she refers to herself as the author. She is, so far, the first identified poet in history, male or female. Her poems chronicle the unstable politics and power plays she witnessed over 4,000 years ago. In her most famous hymn cycle, "Inanna Exalted," she glorified the deeds of her kingly father and praised the moon goddess, Inanna.

Louise Erdrich (1954–)

Novelist, poet, short-story writer

LOUISE ERDRICH'S WRITINGS PORTRAY LIFE IN A fictional part of North Dakota that resembles the town where she grew up. Like many of her characters, Erdrich is a mixed-blood Native American; her father was a German immigrant, and her mother was three-quarters Chippewa.

Erdrich graduated with a B.A. in creative writing from Dartmouth College in 1976 and an M.A. from Johns Hopkins University in 1979. She returned to Dartmouth in 1981 as writer-in-residence and married Michael Dorris, the director of Native American Studies at that time. For the next few years, Erdrich published the stories that would form the groundwork for the first novel in her famous tetralogy.

Erdrich's award-winning story, "The World's Greatest Fishermen," became the opening chapter of

Love Medicine (1984). *The Beet Queen* (1986), *Tracks* (1988), and *Bingo Palace* (1994) followed the same and other characters, chronicling their struggles from 1912 to the present.

In addition to her best-selling novels, Erdrich has published collections of poetry and folktales, as well as *The Crown of Columbus* (1991), a collaboration with her late husband.

Oriana Fallaci (1930–)

Journalist, interviewer, novelist

ORIANA FALLACI HAS WRITTEN ON SUBJECTS ranging from the wonder of space exploration to life in war-torn Beirut. She has published several novels and conducted interviews with such world-famous figures as Indira Gandhi, Golda Meir, and Henry Kissinger. She is best known for her spirited and opinionated approach to her subjects.

Growing up in Florence, Italy, Fallaci's life was deeply affected by the terror of World War II. Her father was a resistance fighter who was imprisoned and tortured for his activism. After the war, the 16-year-old Fallaci enrolled in medical school at the University of Florence. In order to pay her tuition, she began to write for an Italian magazine, *L'Europeo*.

Soon she was selling her stories to international publications, and she left school to write full-time. In her successful book, *If the Sun Dies* (1966), Fallaci presented interviews with astronauts along with her own thoughts about space exploration. Her novel, *Nothing, and So Be It* (1972), is based on her experiences during the Vietnam War. More recently, she published *Inshallah* (1992), a novel that takes place in the bombed-out city of Beirut.

Jessie Redmon Fauset (1882–1961)

Writer, editor, teacher

As literary editor of the NAACP's magazine, *The Crisis*, Jessie Redmon Fauset nurtured such writers as Langston Hughes, Jean Toomer, and Countee Cullen—participants in the "Harlem Renaissance" of the 1920s. She was also the most prolific writer of the era, publishing four novels and numerous essays and stories.

Born into a cultured Philadelphia family, Fauset was the first black woman to graduate Phi Beta Kappa from Cornell University. She taught at an all-black high school in Washington, D.C., before moving to New York City in 1919 to work at *The Crisis*. Her association with W. E. B. Du Bois, the magazine's founder and a leader in the Pan-African movement, was a long one. The indispensable Fauset wrote his speeches, provided translation services at international events, and managed the magazine. She also wrote for and edited *The Brownies' Book*, a children's publication.

A sophisticated, versatile thinker, Fauset wrote fiction, criticism, book reviews, travel essays, and translated works from French. Her novels, which include *Plum Bun* (1929) and *Comedy: American Style* (1933), portrayed the life she knew and were populated with middle-class black people—educated, idealistic, and productive. Some accused her of representing too narrow a portion of black life, but she never ignored racial discrimination. Her books are still worth reading for their elegance of form and thematic concerns.

A Golden Age in Harlem

During the 1920s, African Americans from across the nation were drawn to a neighborhood in New York City called Harlem, where a closely knit artistic community had formed. Jazz composed by black musicians attracted crowds of listeners, black and white. Painters were able to sell their work. Writers celebrated black culture, demanded social change, and still found publishers for their books. Some were troubled by demands made by white patrons, but often this discontent found creative expression in their writing. The advent of the Depression after the disastrous stock market crash of 1929 brought an end to the era, later dubbed the Harlem Renaissance.

Edna Ferber (1885–1968)

Playwright, novelist

Edna Ferber was born in Kalamazoo, Michigan, to a poor Jewish family. By the end of her life, she had been a best-selling writer for over 50 years. More than 20 movies had been made from adaptations of her novels, stories, and plays. It is not surprising that her own realization of the American

dream—the classic rags-to-riches progress of a strong-minded woman—inspired most of her work.

When Ferber was a child, her family moved around the Midwest and often encountered anti-Semitism, an experience she later decided had made her stronger. She dreamed of going to college, but her family's financial situation made this impossible. Instead she became a journalist and began to develop skills of observation that proved useful when she turned to fiction.

After the publication of *Buttered Side Down* (1912), a collection of stories, Ferber's appeal grew steadily. She won the Pulitzer Prize for *So Big* (1924), a novel about Selina Peake DeJong, the daughter of a gambler and a farmer's wife, whose dignity and exceptional character shine in her rugged surroundings. Other novels did equally well, among them *Show Boat* (1926), which was adapted into a hit musical for both stage and screen, and *Giant* (1952), which became an epic film.

Mary Frances Kennedy Fisher (1908–1992)

Food writer, travel writer, memoirist

M. F. K. Fisher grew up in Whittier, a small California town. She was eager to escape those limited surroundings and explore the world. She married Alfred Fisher in 1929, and the couple lived for three years in Dijon, France. Fisher loved the simple life there, especially the fresh, hearty peasant dishes. Back in California, she began to research and write about food. *Serve It Forth* (1937) appeared before the publishers knew that "M. F. K." Fisher was a woman. When she finally visited her editors, they were shocked—women know how to prepare food, they thought, not write about it. Nevertheless, she went on to have a long career as a food writer, producing such successes as *Consider the Oyster* (1941), *The Gastronomical Me* (1943), and *A Cordiall Water* (1961).

Fisher's own life was at times tumultuous. She divorced Albert Fisher and married twice more. Rather than discuss personal hardships in her writing, though, she spoke in symbolic terms. She said, "when I write about hunger, I am really writing about love and the hunger for it, and warmth and the love of it . . . and then the warmth and richness and fine reality of hunger satisfied."

Louise Fitzhugh (1928–1974)

Children's writer, illustrator

Louise Fitzhugh is most recognized for her poignant look at the lives and anxieties of the privileged, but often neglected, children of professional urban parents. Readers continue to identify and sympathize with the difficult lessons learned by the young sleuth Harriet, Fitzhugh's best known character.

Born in Memphis, Tennessee, Fitzhugh attended a variety of colleges and studied painting at the Art Students League both in New York and in Italy. In 1963 she exhibited her oil paintings at a few galleries in New York. Then she turned to writing, producing *Harriet the Spy* (1964) and its sequel, *The Long Secret* (1965). She immediately received praise for her work. *Harriet the Spy* received a Notable Book citation from the American Library Association in 1967. She went on to write and illustrate a number of other children's books before her untimely death in 1974.

María Irene Fornés (1930–)

Experimental playwright

María Irene Fornés came to New York City from Havana, Cuba, in 1945, following the death of her father. She helped the family to make ends meet by taking on a variety of odd jobs. Originally interested in painting, she studied in Italy for three years before returning to New York in 1957. For a while, she supported herself as a textile designer; then, influenced by her roommate, Susan Sontag, Fornés became infatuated with writing. She published her first play, *The Widow*, in 1960, and the next year it was produced Off-Broadway. Unexpectedly, at the age of 30, Fornés had found her true calling, and she has not stopped writing since.

Fornés went on to direct plays, too, and helped to found New York Theatre Strategy to produce new experimental works. She has received dozens of honors, including six Obie awards; prestigious grants have made many of her productions possible. The best known of her plays is probably *Fefu and Her Friends* (1977). While Fornés's work is experimental and ranges in subject matter and style, she has consistently worked to express the concerns of women and of the Latino culture. She is an influential figure in New York's Off-Broadway theater world.

Anne Frank (1929–1945)

Diarist

ANNE FRANK'S STORY IS KNOWN THE WORLD OVER. Her *Diary of a Young Girl* has touched millions with its message of hope and its expression of a 13-year-old girl's longings for life, love, and sanity in a murderous world.

Anne was born in Germany. Because they were Jewish, Otto and Edith Frank decided to move their family to Amsterdam in 1934 to escape Hitler's increasingly powerful Nazi party. But the Germans invaded Holland in 1940, and two years later the Frank family was forced into hiding. Living with several other Jews in a "secret annex" above Otto's factory, they were protected by a few faithful employees, especially Miep Gies. When they were betrayed in 1944, the family was deported to Auschwitz concentration camp. Their mother soon died, and Anne and her sister, Margot, were transferred to Bergen-Belsen. By the time the camp was liberated in 1945, both had died of typhus.

Otto Frank alone survived. After the war, he returned to Amsterdam where he saw Miep Gies again. Among the papers she had saved from the annex was Anne's diary, which Otto published in an edited form in 1947. A 1995 English translation provides the complete work. In the diary, Anne wrote that she wanted to be a journalist; her ambition was nobly if tragically realized.

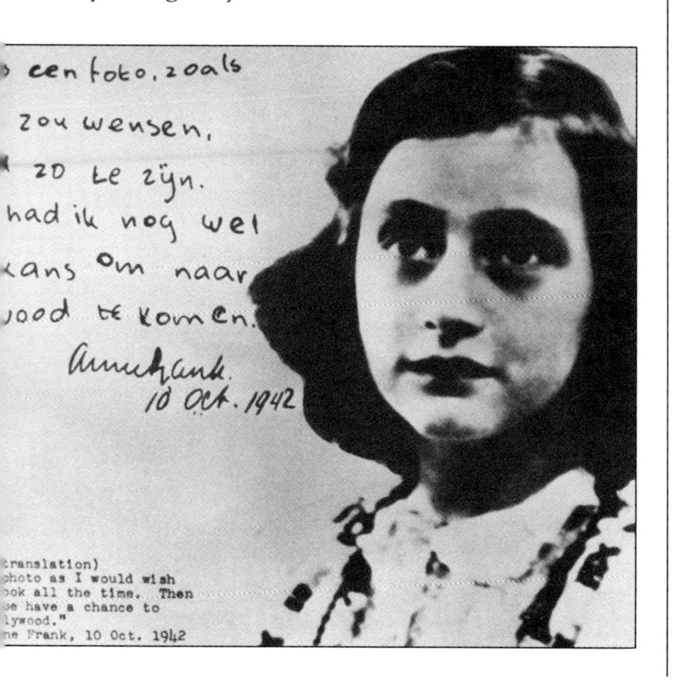

Stella Maria Sarah Miles Franklin (1879–1954)

Novelist

THE AUSTRALIAN NOVELIST MILES FRANKLIN WAS 16 years old when she wrote her masterpiece, *My Brilliant Career.* Determined to see her novel in print, she sent it to many publishers before a British company accepted it in 1901. Critics raved over her semi-autobiographical story of a girl's struggle to break free of woman's traditional role and leave the rough outback. Unfortunately, Franklin's relatives thought her depiction of pioneer families ridiculed them. Their reaction was so negative that Franklin left Australia in 1905. For nearly 30 years, she lived in America and England, became a suffragist, and wrote novels about the outback using a pseudonym, Brent of Bin Bin.

Finally Franklin returned home and resumed writing under her own name. In 1946 she published *My Career Goes Bung*, a sequel to *My Brilliant Career*. She had written it decades before, hoping that the story—in which the heroine returns to her pioneer home—would appease her family. Franklin's books fell out of print, but *My Brilliant Career* was rediscovered by feminist scholars after her death. It became a best-seller in 1965 and inspired an internationally acclaimed film in 1980.

Margaret Fuller (1810–1850)

Writer, feminist, radical

MARGARET FULLER WROTE BRILLIANTLY ABOUT history, social injustice, and equality for women. Her book *Woman in the 19th Century* (1845) inspired the Seneca Falls Women's Convention of 1848.

A daughter of the Boston intellectual aristocracy, Fuller was renowned for her genius and her lively—occasionally intimidating—conversational abilities. During the 1830s, she joined the Transcendentalist circle that included Ralph Waldo Emerson, Bronson Alcott, and Elizabeth Peabody. She was the first woman to edit the Transcendentalist *Dial* magazine. An inspiring teacher, Fuller led "Conversations" about art, music, ethics, and mythology with Boston women. She also attracted the attention of Horace

Greeley, who hired her to write for his newspaper, the *New York Tribune*. When she decided to go abroad in 1846, Greeley made her a foreign correspondent, the first American woman to hold such a position.

In Europe, Fuller befriended George Sand, the poet Adam Mickiewicz, and the radical Giuseppe Mazzini. She met and married Marchese Giovanni Angelo d'Ossolo in Rome and worked with him for Italian freedom while filing reports for the *Tribune*. After the Roman Republic failed in 1850, the couple sailed for America with their son. Only a few miles from their destination, the ship foundered at Fire Island, New York, and the family was drowned.

Charlotte Perkins Gilman (1860–1935)

Feminist writer, lecturer

IN HER SHORT STORY, "THE YELLOW WALL-PAPER" (1892), Charlotte Perkins Gilman tells of a young mother immobilized by melancholy. Rest and total dedication to domestic life are prescribed—with disastrous results. Gilman herself had tried a similar "cure." It nearly drove her mad. Then Gilman visited California alone, and her depression eased. In the end, she and her husband agreed to divorce, and she entrusted him with the care of their daughter.

Gilman, a great-niece of Harriet Beecher Stowe, was born in Hartford, Connecticut. Her childhood was difficult. Abandoned by her father, the family lived on the charity of one relative after another. Nevertheless, she educated herself and was determined to make a difference. In 1888 Gilman moved to California, began writing, and lectured on social reform. In particular, she criticized the idea that women were sexual objects, unpaid domestic servants, and childbearers, not human beings who should be socially and politically active. Her landmark work, *Women and Economics* (1898), attracted widespread attention and influenced the cause of women's rights.

Gilman moved to New York City in 1900 with her second husband and continued her work. Between 1909 and 1916, she wrote and published a feminist magazine, *The Forerunner.* A pacifist, she worked with Jane Addams to establish the Women's Peace Party. At age 75, suffering from breast cancer, she took her own life to avoid being a burden on her daughter.

Susan Glaspell (1882–1948)

Playwright, novelist

AFTER GRADUATING FROM COLLEGE IN IOWA, Susan Glaspell first worked as a journalist and published stories and novels. She was introduced to theater by her husband, George Cram Cook, whom she married in 1913. The couple lived in several American cities, always associating with other writers who were looking for ways to present social issues in their art.

In 1915, while spending the summer with friends in Provincetown, Massachusetts, Glaspell and Cook decided to open a theater to focus on new American plays. The company, which they called the Provincetown Players, performed in Massachusetts for a year before moving to Greenwich Village in New York.

Glaspell's first play, the one-act *Trifles* (1916), was acclaimed for its use of experimental theater techniques. Keeping the central character offstage, Glaspell made effective use of silences in the dialogue and addressed a most untraditional subject: a woman's anger in response to domestic violence. For the next 15 years, Glaspell wrote, directed, and acted for the successful Provincetown Players.

In 1930 Glaspell wrote her Pulitzer Prize–winning play, *Alison's House*, based on the life of

Emily Dickinson. After this she published mostly novels, partly because Cook, her companion in theater work, had died in 1924. Glaspell lived in Provincetown until her own death in 1948.

Nadine Gordimer (1923–)

Novelist, short-story writer

NADINE GORDIMER WON THE NOBEL PRIZE FOR Literature in 1991, honoring her body of work as well as her committed stance against apartheid. Her writings were once banned by the white South African government; her comings and goings were monitored. But, even after she married and had children, Gordimer always refused to go into exile. Outspoken in her condemnation of censorship, she was a founder of the Congress of South African Writers and supported the African National Congress.

Gordimer belonged to a middle-class family of Jewish immigrants who settled near Johannesburg. She never liked school much, but she was an avid reader, and she wrote her first story when she was nine. Her highly praised novels, which include *A Guest of Honour* (1970), *Burger's Daughter* (1979), and *The House Gun* (1998), revolve around questions of personal identity at odds with a racist society. Her writer's voice is calm and unsentimental as it reveals her characters' painful, often deadly, experiences. She is also admired for her mastery of the short story and has published numerous collections, including *Friday's Footprint and Other Stories* (1960).

Today Gordimer travels frequently, lecturing and teaching in the United States and elsewhere. She continues to live in Johannesburg.

Sarah Josepha Hale (1788–1879)

Editor, writer

EDUCATED BY HER MOTHER, BROTHER, AND husband, Sarah Josepha Hale was well prepared to become America's first great female editor. After her husband's death in 1822, she was left with five children to support, so she began writing to earn money. She began by publishing poetry in magazines, and a novel, *Northwood* (1827), followed. Her fiction was not particularly remarkable—she is best known for the famous nursery rhyme "Mary Had a Little Lamb"—but it initiated Hale's career as a magazine editor.

In 1828 Hale became editor of *American Ladies' Magazine*, later renamed *Godey's Lady's Book*. A patriot and a strong supporter of education for women, she often used the magazine as a platform for her own views. Hale fought for recognition of Thanksgiving as a national holiday, and strongly advocated government-funded schools for women. Although she was outspoken about her belief in equal education, she did not ally herself with the feminist movement. Her primary goal was always to promote fellow authors, especially women. She remained editor of *Godey's* until she was 89, and died only two years after her retirement.

Lorraine Vivian Hansberry (1930–1965)

Playwright, civil rights activist

IN 1938 LORRAINE HANSBERRY'S MIDDLE-CLASS black parents bought a home in a restricted neighborhood of Chicago. Well educated and politically active, they intended to force the American justice system to support their right to live there. They ultimately succeeded, but it was a difficult fight. At one point, a brick was even hurled through

their window, almost hitting young Lorraine. Her father took his case—now famous among legal scholars as *Hansberry v. Lee*—all the way to the Supreme Court before he won his point.

The experience helped to inspire Hansberry's 1959 masterpiece, the play *A Raisin in the Sun*. It ran for 530 performances on Broadway and won a New York Drama Critics Circle Award. Hansberry, suddenly a celebrity, used her status to promote the civil rights movement. By the time her next work, *The Sign in Sidney Brustein's Window* (1964), came to the stage, she had been diagnosed with cancer. The play received lukewarm reviews and closed on the night of her death in January 1965.

Because Hansberry died so young, she is known primarily for *Raisin*. However, as a journalist in the early 1950s, she also wrote nonfiction, especially for *Freedom* magazine, which was founded by the singer and activist Paul Robeson. After Hansberry's death, her ex-husband, Robert Nemiroff, published her plays and edited an anthology, *To Be Young, Gifted, and Black: Lorraine Hansberry in Her Own Words* (1969).

Barbara Grizzuti Harrison (1934–)

Journalist, essayist

When Barbara Grizzuti Harrison was in high school, an English teacher told her she would become a writer. It seemed unlikely at the time. Growing up in an Italian family in Brooklyn, New York, Harrison was nine years old when she and her mother joined the Jehovah's Witnesses. The Witnesses valued religious community and required strict self-discipline. Individual creativity was discouraged.

Harrison left the faith when she was in her early 20s. She was married for eight years, had two children, and lived abroad. In 1968 her children's school implemented a feminist curriculum, and Harrison's account of the process was published in the *New Republic* magazine. She then expanded the article into a book, *Unlearning the Lie: Sexism in School* (1969).

Since then, Harrison has published articles, interviews, nonfiction books, and a novel, *Foreign Bodies* (1984). Her investigative journalism is often autobiographical. In 1978 she wrote about her childhood in *Visions of Glory: A History and a Memory of Jehovah's Witnesses*. Harrison travels frequently but continues to make her home in Brooklyn.

Lillian Hellman (1905–1984)

Playwright, memoirist

Lillian Hellman, famous for her suspenseful dramas and outspoken personality, claimed that she disliked the theater. But, after working in publishing, then reading manuscripts for plays and films, she tried her hand at writing a play and produced the hit *The Children's Hour.* It opened in 1934, ran for 691 performances, and was adapted for film. Hellman's reputation for creating vivid female characters and tightly crafted plots was made. Among the many successes that followed were *The*

> **Mrs. Mortar:** You may put that book away, Peggy. I am sure your family need never worry about your going on the stage.
>
> **Peggy:** I don't want to go on the stage. I want to be a lighthouse-keeper's wife.
>
> **Mrs. Mortar:** Well, I certainly hope you won't read to him.
>
> **Lillian Hellman**
> ***The Children's Hour*, Act 1, scene 1**

Little Foxes (1939), *Watch on the Rhine* (1941), and *Toys in the Attic* (1960).

Hellman also had a lifelong interest in politics and was accused by the House Committee on Un-American Activities of supporting communism. She was blacklisted in Hollywood in the 1950s and as a result was prevented from writing screenplays, an important source of income for her.

In the late 1960s, Hellman returned to the public eye when she began publishing her memoirs. The books, which include *An Unfinished Woman* (1969) and *Pentimento* (1973), received tremendous acclaim and aroused new controversy. Some acquaintances, particularly Mary McCarthy, vehemently disputed her accounts of events. Hellman's literary reputation remained high even after her death in 1984.

Josephine Frey Herbst (1892–1969)

Novelist, journalist

JOSEPHINE HERBST, BORN IN SIOUX CITY, IOWA, HAD always planned to be a writer. Financial hardship slowed her progress through college, but she finally graduated from the University of California at Berkeley in 1918. Within two years she had established herself in the radical literary circles of New York City. From 1922 to 1924, she lived in Europe, where she met her husband, John Herrmann.

During the 1930s Herbst experienced her most productive phase. Her famous novel trilogy—*Pity Is Not Enough* (1933), *The Executioner Waits* (1934), and *Rope of Gold* (1939)—is a panoramic, autobiographical chronicle of an American family that covers the period from the Civil War through 1920. An intrepid journalist, Herbst wrote about American farmers' strikes, traveled to Cuba to investigate the growing revolutionary movement there, and went undercover in Germany to meet Nazi Resistance fighters. In 1937, when the Spanish Civil War was in full force, Herbst made sure she was in Madrid to cover it.

In 1940 Herbst's marriage ended, and she suffered increasing pressure from the American government for her leftist politics. Her productivity slowed, although she continued to write, publishing the acclaimed novel, *Hunter of the Dove* (1954), and her memoirs. The Pennsylvania farmhouse where she lived until her death became a meeting place for her many fellow writers and friends.

Hildegard of Bingen (1098–1179)

Poet, mystic, composer

HILDEGARD BEGAN HAVING THE VISIONS THAT guided her extraordinary life when she was a child. She entered a Benedictine order for nuns at age 15, and in 1136 she became abbess (a superior to the nuns). Five years later, her amazing creativity burst forth, and she began to record her visions, eventually filling three volumes. She also wrote about medicine and natural sciences, biographies of saints, music and words for hymns, and letters. Her first book, *Scivias* (Know the ways), contains 26 visions explaining her view of the universe, the nature of the soul, and mortality. The last of the visions includes 14 songs and the earliest known morality play, *Ordo virtutum* (The play of the virtues).

Hildegard's existence over 800 years ago seems miraculous. She was a mystic, poet, doctor, musician, dramatist, and political scholar. She corresponded with powerful leaders—popes, bishops, kings—as well as with monks, nuns, and peasants. She brought her teachings to people far from her home, traveling in Germany, France, Switzerland, and Belgium.

Around 1150, Hildegard had a vision calling her to establish an independent convent for women. This radical idea was at first opposed by male authorities, but she persuaded them to relent. Hildegard then built a convent near Bingen, Germany, where she lived until her death. Today her music is available in recording, and her writings have been translated from the Latin. Many people are moved by her sense of the spirituality of life.

bell hooks (1952–)

Feminist writer

GLORIA JEAN WAS ONE OF SEVEN CHILDREN IN THE Watkins family of Hopkinsville, Kentucky. They were a closely knit group, with a fondness for language. It is not surprising that Gloria became a writer or that she honored her heritage by taking her great-grandmother's name, Bell Hooks, as a pseudonym. To show that she rejects the idea that the author is all-knowing, she usually spells it without capital letters. Her respect for community and her childhood experience of segregation shaped her academic interests. She began by examining black women's place in the feminist movement and went on to consider the ways American popular culture reflects a society that still considers whiteness superior.

Hooks began her first book, *Ain't I a Woman: Black Women and Feminism* as a 19-year-old undergraduate at Stanford University. It was published in 1981, after she received her Ph.D. A prolific writer, she has published numerous magazine articles as well as books. Among her works are *Black Looks: Race and Representation* (1992) and *Bone Black: Memories of Girlhood* (1996). She is also a committed teacher and has been a professor at several schools, including Yale University and Oberlin College.

Zora Neale Hurston (1891–1960)

Novelist, folklorist, short-story writer

IN HER AUTOBIOGRAPHY, *DUST TRACKS ON A ROAD* (1942), Zora Neale Hurston describes her childhood in Eatonville, Florida, the country's first all-black town, where her father was mayor. Tragically, her mother, who always encouraged her to "jump at de sun," died when Hurston was nine. Five years later, she left Florida. Mystery surrounds the next few years, which she never wrote about. In fact, she later claimed to be ten years younger than she was, perhaps because she had resumed her education and wanted to blend in with the other students. Hurston enrolled at Howard University in 1918. There her writings were noticed by Alain Locke, who was active in the Harlem Renaissance.

Hurston moved to New York City and became friends with other black writers. Fun-loving and flamboyant, she loved to shock people with her extravagant behavior. But she was also a scholar, studying with the anthropologist Franz Boas at Barnard College and traveling to the South to document black folk stories, music, and voodoo spells. *Mules and Men* (1935) is an invaluable collection of folklore, and most of her fiction has a folkloric element.

Hurston's celebration of black culture led her to adopt some conservative political views—she opposed the desegregation of schools, for example. The writer Richard Wright was among those who criticized her, saying she ignored discrimination against blacks.

Hurston's masterful novel, *Their Eyes Were Watching God* (1937), is widely read today. Still, much of her work was never published, and she fell into obscurity during the 1950s, dying penniless.

Inez Haynes Irwin (1873–1970)

Feminist historian, novelist

INEZ IRWIN WAS AT HIGH SCHOOL IN BOSTON WHEN her teacher assigned her to write an essay on the topic "Should women vote?" Her passionate pro-suffrage composition became the first of many writings in favor of women's rights.

While she was a student at Radcliffe College in the late 1890s, she befriended Maud Wood Park, one of the few young women there who shared her feminist views. Together they founded the College Equal Suffrage League. After graduation, she moved to New York City and immersed herself in the Greenwich Village intellectual scene. There she wrote fiction and worked as story editor for the radical paper *The Masses*. Her novels included the feminist *Lady of the Kingdoms* (1917) and *Gideon* (1927), a tale of divorce.

Irwin's political activity brought her to historical writing, her greatest talent. *The Story of the Woman's Party* (1921) is a documentary-style history of Alice Paul's National Woman's party. She also published *Angels and Amazons: A Hundred Years of American Women* in 1933.

Her second marriage, to the journalist William Henry Irwin, was an especially happy one. Soon after his death in 1948, she retired from writing.

Shirley Jackson (1919–1963)

Novelist, short-story writer

SHIRLEY JACKSON'S MOST FAMOUS SHORT STORY, "The Lottery," was first published in the *New Yorker* magazine in 1948. The events described—townspeople gather to draw lots for a purpose that only gradually becomes clear—seem normal enough at first. But the sense of foreboding grows steadily, until it becomes gripping terror.

A Californian, Jackson moved to New York State during high school. She met her husband, Stanley Hyman, while they were both students at the University of Syracuse. Hyman quickly established himself as a literary critic and then took a job teaching at Bennington College in Vermont. Jackson wrote humorously about being a professor's wife and the mother of four children in *Life Among the Savages* (1953), and *Raising Demons* (1957).

Those wholesome works are altogether different from the eerie mixture of fantasy and realism that pervades her novels and stories. Jackson, who was herself plagued by numerous phobias, often wrote about women whose worlds unexpectedly turn from normal to nightmarish. In her best novels, *The Haunting of Hill House* (1959) and *We Have Always Lived in the Castle* (1962), she combines the grotesque and the comic, the ordered and the disturbed.

Sarah Orne Jewett (1849–1909)

Novelist

BY THE TIME SARAH ORNE JEWETT WAS BORN IN South Berwick, Maine, the shipping industry had long since abandoned the state, leaving many people unemployed. Her great-grandfather had made a fortune as a shipowner, so the Jewetts were wealthy, but the towns surrounding their home were shabby and desolate. As a girl, Jewett accompanied her physician father as he tended his patients. She observed everything closely; these seaside communities became the inspiration for her work.

Jewett's first story, "Jenny Garrow's Lovers," appeared in a publication called *The Flag of Our Union* three years after she graduated from high school, launching her career. Soon national magazines, such as the *Atlantic Monthly* and *Harper's*, requested stories from her, too. In 1877 she reworked some of her writings and assembled them into a book, *Deephaven*. Numerous other books followed, most notably *The Country of Pointed Firs* (1896).

Jewett was a sociable, well-traveled woman. She knew many literary stars of her day, both in America and abroad. Nevertheless, she found deep meaning in ordinary life and continued to write about small-town Maine. Her work influenced other early 20th-century women writers, most notably Willa Cather.

In 1902 a near-fatal accident ended Jewett's writing career. She died seven years later in the house where she was born.

Sor Juana Inés de la Cruz (1651–1695)

Lyric poet, playwright, scholar

Juana Inés de la Cruz learned to read at age three and write by the time she was five. She composed a dramatic poem at eight, mastered Latin at nine, and astounded forty professors in Mexico City with her learning at 17.

The daughter of a Spanish military officer and a Creole mother, Juana had begged them to let her dress as a boy and go to university, but they refused. For a time, she was a member of the court kept by the Spanish governor, or viceroy. She composed poems for special occasions, displaying a knowledge of mathematics, art, music, physics, and theology. Beautiful as well as brilliant, she attracted many admirers.

Intent on living a scholarly life, she entered the convent of Saint Jerome rather than marry. During the next 23 years, Sor Juana won international reknown for her poetry, philosophical writings, and scientific investigations.

Increasingly, however, she was condemned by her religious superiors for believing that women had the right to develop their minds as well as their souls. At last, after writing an autobiographical defense of women's rights and the poem "Foolish Men Who Accuse Women," she submitted. Signing a confession in blood and selling her library of 4,000 books, Sor Juana dedicated herself to religious duties after 1693. She died nursing her convent sisters during an epidemic.

Julian of Norwich (1342–after 1416)

Mystical poet

Julian of Norwich is the first Englishwoman whose signed writings have survived. Unfortunately, little is known of her life, and even the name we have for her is a pseudonym. She lived in a small dwelling attached to the church of St. Julian in Norwich. An anchoress, or religious hermit, she read widely, offered spiritual teaching and comfort to passersby, and wrote two versions of her book, *Revelations of Divine Love.* The *Revelations* are considered among the greatest works of Medieval mysticism. Julian has been praised as much for the depth of her religious understanding as for her beautiful language.

On May 13, 1373, Julian suddenly recovered from a terrible and extended illness after experiencing 16 visions of the Virgin Mary and Jesus. Her cure was, she was convinced, a divine call to write down what she had seen. She wrote an initial version of the *Revelations.* For the next two decades, she devoted herself to study and further contemplations about her experiences. Then she revised and expanded her original writings.

"And then our good Lord opened my ghostly eye, and shewed me my soul in the midst of my heart. I saw the soul so large as it were an endless world, and also as it were a blessed kingdom. And by the conditions that I saw therein, I understood that it is a worshipful city."

Julian of Norwich
Revelations of Divine Love

Interesting for religious scholars today is Julian of Norwich's reexamination of patriarchal images of God, particularly in the idea of the "mothering" Jesus, whose sacrifice she compares with a mother's sacrifice for her children. Julian felt called to bring tidings of human salvation. As she assures the reader, "all shall be well, and all shall be well, and all manner of things shall be well."

Pauline Kael (1919–)

Film critic

PAULINE KAEL'S FATHER WAS A MOVIE FAN, AND she inherited his enthusiasm to an even greater degree. Raised in San Francisco, Kael studied philosophy at the University of California at Berkeley. After graduating, she worked at odd jobs while trying her hand at filmmaking, writing plays, and then reviewing.

In 1953 a small San Francisco magazine, *City Lights*, published her first film review. She went on to write reviews for various publications, broadcast them on radio, and run one of the first theaters featuring art films. These early efforts brought her little or no pay. Finally, Kael received national recognition with her best-selling collection of reviews, *I Lost It at the Movies* (1965).

Moving to New York City, Kael had become a staff reviewer for the *New Yorker* magazine by 1968. She was known for her wit and her firm refusal to allow popular sentiment to influence her—she panned the film *The Sound of Music*. She once wrote that, "the words 'Kiss Kiss Bang Bang,' which I saw on an Italian movie poster, are perhaps the briefest statement imaginable of the basic appeal of movies."

Kael made quite a stir in 1971 when her introduction to the *Citizen Kane Book* questioned the belief that Orson Welles was the sole creative genius behind the film *Citizen Kane*. She retired from the *New Yorker* in 1991.

Maxine Kumin (1925–)

Poet, novelist, children's writer

MAXINE KUMIN GREW UP IN PHILADELPHIA, where her father was a pawnbroker. Although her family was Jewish, they were not religious, and she attended Catholic schools. She began writing poetry when she was eight, but her first focused interest was swimming—she even trained for the Olympics. Giving that idea up, she enrolled at Radcliffe College in Massachusetts, where she earned her bachelor's and master's degrees. She was still a student when she married Victor Kumin in 1946.

Kumin spent the time after her graduation caring for her son and two daughters and did not publish her first volume of poetry, *Halfway*, until 1961. Once started though, she produced a steady stream of books, both poetry and novels. She has written over 20 children's stories, four of which were collaborations with her friend Anne Sexton. In 1973 Kumin received the Pulitzer Prize for her poetry collection *Up Country*.

Maxine Kumin's poetry is detailed and autobiographical. Farm life, her relationship with her children, and her friendship with Sexton are all represented in her work. Kumin and her husband raise horses on the New Hampshire farm where they have lived since 1976, and she continues to be inspired by her life there. In 1994 she published *Women, Animals, and Vegetables*, a collection of essays and stories about rural life.

Selma Lagerlöf (1858–1940)

Novelist

IN 1909 SELMA LAGERLÖF MADE HISTORY AS THE first woman and first Swede to receive the Nobel Prize for Literature. Among the works for which she was honored were *Jerusalem* (1901–1902) and the two-volume series, *The Wonderful Adventures of Nils* and *Further Adventures of Nils*. The *Nils* books recall her happy childhood in the rural town of Marbacka, where storytelling was a frequent pastime. Lagerlöf used her prize money to buy her beloved childhood home.

Trained as a teacher, Lagerlöf became a schoolmistress in 1885 and wrote stories for magazines in her spare time. Her first novel, *The Gösta Berling Saga* (1891), attracted critics' attention. By 1895 she had won a travel scholarship and was able to concentrate on writing. She steadily gained in prominence and was honored in 1914 by being the first woman granted membership in the Swedish Academy, an organization that promotes Swedish culture and also administers the Nobel Prize.

World War I had a profound, distressing effect on her, stifling her impulse to write. Afterward, she published such autobiographical pieces as *Marbacka* (1922) and *Memories of My Childhood* (1930). In the last year of her life, Lagerlöf arranged for the Jewish poet Nelly Sachs to leave Nazi Germany and settle in Sweden.

Harper Lee (1926–)

Novelist

HARPER LEE'S ONLY BOOK HAS BECOME A CLASSIC of American literature, still widely read nearly 40 years after it first appeared. Lee, whose father was a lawyer, was born in Monroeville, Alabama. Her childhood in that small southern town inspired the story she tells in *To Kill a Mockingbird.*

Narrated by Jean Louisa Finch, known as Scout, the novel follows Scout, her brother, and their summertime friend Dill in a coming-of-age story set over a three-year period. The children witness the persecution of people who are different or powerless in a culture that condemns them without questioning. Scout learns the importance of defending the wrongly accused, both in court, as her lawyer father does, and in everyday life.

In 1961 *To Kill a Mockingbird* won the Pulitzer Prize. Lee went on to help her childhood friend Truman Capote research his book *In Cold Blood* (1965), but she never published another novel. Still, her book, written just before the civil rights movements of the 1960s, continues to teach young people to consider their responsibilities as members of a diverse society.

Ursula Le Guin (1929–)

Science fiction writer

"TRUTH IS A MATTER OF THE IMAGINATION," says Genly Ai, a character in Ursula Le Guin's *The Left Hand of Darkness* (1969). In her science fiction and fantasy stories, Le Guin has sought to unveil truth through vividly imagined places, peoples, and myths. As a Taoist, she infuses her writings with the idea of the unity of all things, whether of opposing forces, or the disparate elements within society and the individual. Beneath external events, a moral framework gives her stories unusual depth, as does her attention to character development and style.

The daughter of a writer and an anthropologist, Le Guin grew up among scholars and the Californian Native Americans whose culture her father studied. She became an academic herself, graduating from Radcliffe College in 1951 and earning a master's degree in literature from Columbia University. While in Europe on a Fulbright scholarship, she met her husband, Charles Le Guin.

Le Guin worked as a French professor, then turned to writing science fiction. She produced such well-known books as *The Dispossessed* (1974) and the four novels that make up the Earthsea cycle: *The Wizard of Earthsea* (1968), *The Tombs of Atuan* (1971), *The Farthest Shore* (1972), and *Tehanu* (1990). Le Guin has received numerous honors, including the Nebula and Hugo awards for authors of science fiction and a Newbery Silver Medal. Since 1959 she has lived in Portland, Oregon.

Madeleine L'Engle (1918–)

Novelist

MADELEINE L'ENGLE WAS THE CHILD OF CULTURED parents who encouraged creativity and moral questioning. Her family lived for a time in Europe, and the experience taught her to love foreign places and customs. One of their homes was a castle that hadn't been renovated in 800 years—a reality as fantastic as fiction. After college, L'Engle returned to her native New York City in 1941 and worked in theater, where she met her husband. Their happy marriage produced three children and lasted 40 years, until his death in 1986.

L'Engle's reputation as a writer grew gradually. Throughout the 1950s, she produced modest successes. The first of a series about a family, *Meet the Austins* (1960), attracted a devoted readership. Meanwhile, she tried to interest publishers in a science fiction book for young adults.

Astonishingly, the now-beloved *A Wrinkle in Time* was rejected 26 times. When it finally appeared in 1962, it won the prestigious Newbery Medal and became a best-seller. She has since published two sequels, *A Wind in the Door* (1973) and *A Swiftly Tilting Planet* (1978), and many other novels and autobiographical works. L'Engle tackles complex and sometimes threatening realities, but always with an underlying optimism that this is a spiritually driven universe where everything is interconnected.

Anna Leonowens (1834–1914)

Journalist, writer, teacher

ANNA LEONOWENS LED AN INDUSTRIOUS AND adventurous life. The daughter of a British army officer, she was born in Wales and moved to India when she was 15. Shortly thereafter, she married the young Major Thomas Leonowens, and they began the traveling life of a military family. They were shipwrecked on their way to England, posted to Australia, transferred to Singapore (then fled because of a rebellion), and returned to India. Thomas died of sunstroke after a tiger hunt in 1859, and Leonowens took her two children to Singapore, where she set up a school.

In 1862 King Mongkut invited her to go to Siam—today Thailand—to educate his 64 children and several of his wives. Her books, *The English Governess at the Siamese Court* (1870) and *The Romance of the Harem* (1872), describe the exotic aspects of court life, but they also express a feminist perspective, denouncing slavery and women's role in the society.

Poor health forced Anna to leave Thailand in 1867. She moved first to the United States, then to Nova Scotia. She continued to write, travel, and devote herself to education and social reform. She remained friends with her former pupil, Prince Chulalongkorn. As a result of her influence, he abolished slavery in Siam when he became king.

Anna in Popular Culture

Today, through romanticized adaptations of her writings about Thailand, Anna Leonowens has become almost more of a fictional character than a historical one. The writer Margaret Landon, inspired by Leonowens's memoirs, published *Anna and the King of Siam* in 1946. That book was adapted into a film. Then the screenplay was transformed into a musical play—*The King and I*—which did so well on the Broadway stage that it was made into another movie in 1956. Yul Brynner played the role of King Mongkut in both the stage and screen versions of the musical.

Gerda Lerner (1920–)

Historian, educator, pioneer of women's studies

IN 1939 GERDA KRONSTEIN AND HER FAMILY FLED Nazi-controlled Austria and settled in the United States. After marrying Karl Lerner in 1941, she began studying American history to understand her new homeland. Lerner was shocked by the absence of women in all the books she read. Investigating further, she found that women had made many great contributions no one had written about. So at age 42, she decided to go to college. Enrolling at the New School for Social Research in New York City, she began teaching women's history even before she received her degree. She was accepted for graduate work at Columbia University, and when she found that no formal women's history program was available, she simply constructed her own.

In 1966 Lerner published her doctoral dissertation, *The Grimké Sisters from South Carolina: Rebels Against Slavery.* She followed with *The Woman in American History* (1971) and an anthology of black women's writings, *Black Women in White America: A Documentary History* (1972). In all her books, she made a point of resurrecting forgotten voices from America's past.

After her retirement in 1991, Lerner published *Why History Matters: Life and Thought*, a compilation of essays. By insisting that history students recognize women's contributions, Lerner has helped make women's studies—once an "exotic" field—part of every university's curriculum.

Doris Lessing (1919–)

Novelist

Doris Lessing, the daughter of a British army officer, was born in Iran and raised in Zimbabwe (then Rhodesia). Unhappy at school, she withdrew when she was 14 years old. By 1938 she was living alone and supporting herself at clerical jobs while writing fiction. She was married twice, briefly, in the 1940s and gave birth to three children. Then, in 1949, she moved to London. Always interested in politics, Lessing was a member of the Communist party for a time and demonstrated against nuclear weapons.

Lessing, a brilliant experimental writer and a visionary, seeks to expand human consciousness as a means of creating social harmony. *The Children of Violence* series (1952–1969) follows her principal character, Martha Quest, through five books as she struggles to understand what it means to be human. In *The Golden Notebook* (1962), a writer named Anna Wulf confronts the modern-day anxieties of racial and sexual prejudice, and personal and political responsibility. With *Canopus in Argos: Archives* (1979–1983), again five volumes, Lessing experimented in what she calls "space fiction."

Lessing then used her writing to demonstrate the difficulties that unknown authors face in the modern publishing world. After publishing two novels under a pseudonym, she collected them in *The Diaries of Jane Somers* (1984) and added a preface that described her experiences. *Walking in the Shade*, the second volume of her memoirs, appeared in 1997.

Denise Levertov (1923–1997)

Poet

Each member of Denise Levertov's family played a part in the development of her creative vision. Her Welsh mother told magical stories from the folklore of England and Wales. Her father, a Russian Jew who became an Episcopalian priest, taught her the Jewish mystical traditions of Hasidic texts. Her beloved sister, Olga, introduced the younger Denise to the wonders of poetry.

The English-born Levertov's first book, *The Double Image*, appeared in 1946. The following year she married the writer Mitchell Goodman, and the pair soon moved to the United States. In America, Levertov came to be associated with poets like William Carlos Williams, H.D., and Robert Creeley through her use of clear language and her variations of rhyme and rhythm. She excelled in expressing emotional and mystical responses to the beauty of the physical world and to her family life.

Levertov's art was also moral. She was horrified by the 20th century's history of conflict, experienced firsthand during World War II, when her parents' London home had been a refuge for Jews fleeing the Nazis. As America entered into wars in Vietnam and Latin America, she participated in protest rallies and stated her opposition to cruelty and injustice in her writing. For a time she was criticized for mingling politics and poetry. Today she is deemed one of our leading literary artists, and poems such as "Life at War" and "During the Eichmann Trial" are considered some of her best.

Li Ch'ing-chao (1081–1150?)

Poet

Li Ch'ing-chao is one of China's most beloved poets, even though only bits and fragments of her work remain—about 50 poems out of 13 volumes of essays and poetry. She wrote *tz'u* poetry, a specific style of short, lyrical verse intended to be accompanied by music. Her work is known for the depth of emotion expressed, and her experimental use of rhythm and rhyme.

Li Ch'ing-chao was born in the Shantung province in China. Her family was a wealthy and literary one. In 1101 she married an art collector named Chao Ming-ch'eng, and the two were very happy together.

In 1127 war struck China, and their settled life took a dramatic turn. They attempted to flee the violence, but Chao Ming-ch'eng died in 1129 while they were on the road. Traveling on alone, Li Ch'ing-chao eventually arrived in the town of Chin-hua, where she lived with her brother until her death.

"... Flowers, after their
Nature, whirl away in the wind.
Spilt water, after its nature,
Flows together at the lowest point.
Those who are of one being
Can never stop thinking of each other.
But, ah, my dear, we are apart,
And I have become used to sorrow.
This love—nothing can ever
Make it fade or disappear.
For a moment it was on my eyebrows,
Now it is heavy in my heart."

Li Ch'ing Chao,
translated by Kenneth Rexroth
from a poem to the tune, "Plum
Blossoms Fall and Scatter"

Clarice Lispector (1925–1977)

Novelist, short-story writer

Clarice Lispector, one of Brazil's most celebrated writers, is known for her intimate psychological examinations of her characters, especially women. Her work, with its focus on the universality of human emotion, was exceptionally modern and international for its time. She became a major influence on Brazilian literature in particular, inspiring authors to move away from their reliance on realism and regional themes.

Although she was born in Chechilnik, a town in the Ukraine, Lispector was raised from infancy in Brazil. In 1943, when she was only 18, she graduated from law school in Rio de Janeiro, finished her first book, and was married. A year later, the novel, *Perto do coração selvagem* (Close to the savage heart), was published, and she and her husband, a diplomat, moved to Europe.

Even though they lived abroad for nearly 20 years, Lispector's literary reputation grew steadily at home. In 1960 she separated from her husband and returned to Rio de Janeiro. Before long Lispector had produced two collections of short stories, *Laços de família* (1960, Family ties) and *A legião estrangeira* (1964, The foreign legion), which brought her international recognition. In addition to her novels and short stories, she also wrote a number of children's stories. Much of her last novel, *Um sopro de vida* (1978, A breath of life), was written after she learned she had terminal cancer.

Anita Loos (1893–1981)
Novelist, playwright, and screenwriter

ANITA LOOS'S PROLIFIC CAREER BEGAN EARLY. Growing up in San Francisco, California, she acted onstage from the age of five. By 13, she was a journalist for the New York *Morning Telegraph* and other periodicals. She sold a film scenario to D. W. Griffith's Biograph Company in 1912, before she had turned 20.

By the time Loos married John Emerson in 1919, she had written for over 200 silent films, providing the storyline, witty subtitles, or both. Hollywood's biggest stars, including Lillian Gish and Mary Pickford, regularly played roles she had dreamed up.

Loos and her husband collaborated on writing projects and began producing their own movies. Meanwhile, she wrote several plays for Broadway and, in 1925, published her most famous novel, *Gentlemen Prefer Blondes.* The satirical portrait of the beautiful, money-driven Lorelei Lee was wildly popular. She went on to adapt the story for both stage and film.

After the 1940s, Loos lived mostly in New York City. In addition to plays, screenplays, adaptations, and novels, she wrote several memoirs about her Hollywood experiences.

Amy Lowell (1874–1925)
Poet, critic

AMY LOWELL WAS A "CHARACTER" IN THE MODERN sense: she was heavy, smoked cigars, and wore debutante's clothes. She slept by day, wrote poetry at night, lived with a woman, and was surrounded by a troop of untrained dogs.

A member of a wealthy, intellectual Boston family, Lowell was educated privately and often traveled abroad. Not until she was 28 did she decide to dedicate herself to poetry and literature, undertaking a disciplined study by herself and becoming both a renowned poet and a poetry critic.

Lowell's first published collection was entitled *A Dome of Many-Colored Glass* (1912). A year later, she met the poet Ezra Pound in London and, through his influence, adopted the style of Imagism, using free verse, everyday language, and precise, concrete imagery to express meaning. Her second book, *Sword Blades and Poppy Seed* (1914), reflected this new style. Her interest in the romantic French poets also affected her work, and she translated several of them into English (*Six French Poets*, 1915). Lowell's final collection of poetry, *What's O'Clock*, was published shortly after her death and received the Pulitzer Prize in 1926.

Mabel Dodge Luhan (1879–1962)

Salon hostess, writer

Mabel Dodge Luhan's memoirs provide a revealing look at the cultural climate of her time. However, she is best known for her role in bringing together and inspiring other artists.

The only child of wealthy parents in Buffalo, New York, Mabel married Karl Evans when she was 21, but he died the next year. To recover from the shock, she traveled to Europe, where she married Edwin Dodge in 1905. The couple's palatial home in Florence, Italy, became a social center for intellectuals living abroad, among them Gertrude Stein. Leaving her husband in 1912, Mabel moved to New York City and established one of America's greatest salons. Emma Goldman, Amy Lowell, and many others were part of her circle. She married again, this time a painter named Maurice Sterne.

Mabel moved to Taos, New Mexico, in 1918. There she found the sense of community she had been searching for all along. Having divorced Sterne to marry Tony Luhan, a Pueblo Indian, she lived in Taos for the rest of her days, making it the site of her most impressive salon yet. Georgia O'Keeffe and D. H. Lawrence were regular visitors. A charismatic, sometimes ruthless, personality, Luhan was not always liked by the intellectuals she gathered around her, but she inspired and encouraged many of them.

Mary McCarthy (1912–1989)

Novelist, critic

Mary McCarthy remembered her earliest years happily, until her parents' death from influenza in 1918. After that, as she describes in *Memories of a Catholic Childhood* (1957), she and her brothers were raised in Minnesota by severe and unloving relatives. McCarthy graduated from Vassar College in 1933 and immersed herself in New York City's intellectual world, working as a book and theater reviewer. In 1938 she married the critic Edmund Wilson, the second of her four husbands.

Wilson encouraged McCarthy to write fiction, and she began by publishing short stories in magazines. Her novel, *The Groves of Academe* (1952), satirized faculty politics. Her most popular novel, *The Group* (1963), was a sardonic look at the lives of eight Vassar-educated women. Two travel books, *Venice Observed* (1956) and *The Stones of Florence* (1959), display her gifts as an observer of art and culture. Always politically engaged, she bluntly criticized Senator Joseph McCarthy as he orchestrated the Communist scare of the 1950s. She expressed her opposition to the Vietnam War in articles and books.

McCarthy's ability to write fiction, criticism, autobiography, travel, and journalism made her one of the foremost women of letters of her time. Her brilliant mind and wicked wit gave her a reputation for intellectual toughness, but she could be a tender and devoted friend. She had an especially warm relationship with the writer Hannah Arendt.

Vassar College

"Like Athena, goddess of wisdom, Vassar College sprang in full battle dress from the head of a man," wrote Mary McCarthy in her essay "The Vassar Girl." Originally a women's college, Vassar was endowed in 1861 by Matthew Vassar of Poughkeepsie, New York, a brewer and self-made man who wanted to assure his name in history. Many graduates have gone on to become famous, living up to his hopes. To mention a few: In addition to Mary McCarthy, the writers Edna St. Vincent Millay and Muriel Rukeyser; the scientists Ellen Swallow Richards and Grace Hopper; the reformers Harriot Stanton Blatch and Julia Clifford Lathrop; the first lady Jacqueline Kennedy Onassis; the newspaper executive Katharine Graham; and the actresses Jane Fonda and Meryl Streep. Vassar became coeducational in 1969.

Carson McCullers (1917–1967)

Novelist, playwright

Carson McCullers was a precocious child with talents for storytelling and music. Growing up in Columbus, Georgia, she received devoted, perhaps overly possessive, encouragement from her mother, who had recognized Carson's gifts early on. At age 17, she moved to New York City to study piano at the Juilliard School of Music. Once there, though, she concentrated more on her writing, producing stories about tormented, lonely souls seeking salvation through love, which was rarely returned. Grotesque situations, crippled men and women, and confused adolescents populate her melancholy tales.

The Heart Is a Lonely Hunter (1940), McCullers's first novel, made her a literary sensation at the age of 23. In the book a deaf-mute man becomes the focus of the other characters' desperate needs for sympathy and love. *The Member of the Wedding* (1946), a novella she also adapted into a play, was her most successful work. The drama ran on Broadway for over a year.

McCullers's difficult marriage, recurrent illnesses, self-destructive drinking, and bouts with despair made their marks on works such as *Reflections in a Golden Eye* (1941), *The Ballad of the Sad Cafe* (1952), and *Clock Without Hands* (1961). A succession of serious health problems distracted her from writing during her last years. She was 50 when she suffered a third, and fatal, stroke.

Harriet Martineau (1802–1876)

Essayist, novelist, economics writer

The Martineau family of Norwich, England, educated all of their children, girls and boys. Harriet in particular showed promise, with her wide curiosity and quick memory. When her beloved brother, James, became a Unitarian, she studied theology and developed her own spiritual philosophy. Although always intellectually active, she suffered from frequent illness, beginning with a loss of hearing, taste, and smell as a girl.

After the stock market crashed in 1825, the family business failed. Forced to earn an income, Martineau turned to writing. With the publication of *Illustrations of Political Economy* (1832–1834), a best-selling series of short stories explaining the principles of economics for general readers, her fortunes improved dramatically.

Martineau toured America from 1834 to 1836 and became an ardent abolitionist. She went on to write prolifically on a wide variety of topics. Her novel *Deerbrook* (1839) was followed by *The Hour and the Man* (1840), about the Haitian president Toussaint L'Ouverture. In 1853 *The Positive Philosophy of Auguste Comte* was praised. Diagnosed with fatal heart disease in 1855, she rushed to write her *Autobiography* (1877). As it turned out, she lived for 20 more years, as productive as ever.

Edna St. Vincent Millay (1892–1950)

Poet, playwright

Beautiful, bohemian, romantic, rebellious, and witty, Edna St. Vincent Millay defined the "liberated" woman poet of the Roaring Twenties. She became famous for her line, "my candle burns at both ends." But deeper than that charismatic image was her passionate dedication to her craft and the independence and honesty of her personal life.

Millay was raised in Maine by her mother, a divorcée who supported her three daughters as a nurse and set an example of strong self-reliance. When she was 20, Millay published the poem "Renascence," which brought her a scholarship to Vassar College. Afterward her interest in theater attracted her to the Provincetown Players in New York City. She became friends with such radicals and writers as Max Eastman, Edmund Wilson, and John Reed.

In her debut poetry collection, *A Few Figs from Thistles* (1920), Millay delighted readers with her spirited assertion of woman's individuality. *The Harp Weaver*, published three years later, demonstrated

her skill at writing sonnets and made her the first female winner of the Pulitzer Prize for poetry. Her most successful work for the stage was the libretto for Deems Taylor's opera *The King's Henchman*.

Always politically active, Millay read a poem at the dedication of the National Woman's party in 1923. She also took part in protesting the notorious case of Nicola Sacco and Bartolomeo Vanzetti, two immigrants executed for murder in 1927.

Gabriela Mistral (1889–1957)

Poet, diplomat, educator

IN 1945 GABRIELA MISTRAL BECAME THE FIRST Latin American woman to win a Nobel Prize. Honored for her contribution to literature, her life as poet was inseparable from her life as teacher and cultural minister. Mistral began teaching in small-town Chilean schools when she was 15. Named Chile's "Teacher of the Nation" in 1923, she promoted educational reform at home and in Mexico. She also served as a diplomat in Europe, Brazil, and at the United Nations in New York.

Born Lucila Godoy Alcayaga, she adopted the name Gabriela Mistral when she published the three poems "Sonnets of Death," which won a prize in Santiago in 1914. Much of her poetry is about loss: abandonment by her father, the deaths of lovers and friends. She wrote often of her unfulfilled desire to be a mother. The pieces in her first collection, *Desolación* (1922, Desolation), express her anguish with characteristic intensity.

In expressing private griefs in her writings, Mistral also spoke for the voiceless people—women and children—she worked to help in her public life.

Lucy Maud Montgomery (1874–1942)

Novelist, children's writer

NEARLY ALL OF L. M. MONTGOMERY'S BOOKS TAKE place on Prince Edward Island in Canada, where she grew up. Her captivating descriptions of the island and its people, as well as her ability to look at the world through a child's eyes, have appealed to generations of young readers.

In spite of her great nostalgia for childhood, Montgomery's own youth was lonely. Raised by her maternal grandparents who gave her little affection, she took refuge in writing stories. As a young woman, she worked as a schoolteacher, then began writing *Anne of Green Gables* (1908). The book became a success worldwide. People were fascinated by the story of the red-headed orphan girl sent to a crotchety old couple who had requested a boy, and how they came to love their strong-minded new daughter.

Montgomery married in 1911 and moved to Leaskdale, Ontario, but continued to write *Anne* books—ten of them in all. In addition, she wrote many other children's books and two novels for adults. She retired from writing a few years before her death.

Marianne Moore (1887–1972)

Poet

MARIANNE MOORE'S PRECISE OBSERVATIONS OF the physical world are infused with the imaginative gift of the poet. In one of her most quoted works, "Poetry," she instructs would-be writers to present "imaginary gardens with real toads in them," advice she consistently followed in her own, highly original, poetry.

After graduating from Bryn Mawr with a degree in biology, Moore taught secretarial courses at the United States Indian School in Carlisle, Pennsylvania.

In 1918 she moved to New York City with her mother, her constant companion for most of her life. Her first book, *Poems*, appeared in 1921. Moore's discipline and craftsmanship won her early favor from fellow poets, and she was soon hired as editor of the *Dial* literary magazine. Her friends and admirers included William Carlos Williams, Wallace Stevens, Ezra Pound, and T. S. Eliot. She eventually earned a following with the general public as well. In 1952 her *Collected Poems* won not only the National Book Award, but the Pulitzer and Bollingen prizes. In 1955 she was inducted into the American Academy of Arts and Letters.

> **"If I, like Solomon, . . .**
> **could have my wish—**
>
> **my wish . . . O to be a dragon,**
> **a symbol of the power of Heaven—of silkworm**
> **size or immense; at times invisible.**
> **Felicitous phenomenon!"**
>
> **Marianne Moore**
> **"O to Be a Dragon," 1959**

After her mother's death in 1947, Moore, who had been living in Brooklyn, returned to Manhattan. There her black tricorn hat and cape and her fascination with exotic animals, sports, and ballet made her a public celebrity. She even appeared on television talk shows before her death at the age of 84.

Toni Morrison (1931–)

Novelist, critic, educator

Toni Morrison—born Chloe Anthony Wofford—grew up in Ohio. Although they were not well-off, the Woffords encouraged their children to be proud and ambitious. Chloe's father worked three jobs to support his family. Her mother's musical gifts and her grandmother's tales of the supernatural and African American folklore inspired the budding scholar and writer. After earning her B.A. from Howard University and a master's degree from Cornell, she began teaching. She married architect Harold Morrison and had two sons before they were divorced in 1964.

In 1965 Morrison became a senior editor at Random House. Concerned that so little work by black writers was being published, she made an effort to promote them. Before she left the job in 1983, she worked on books by such writers as Toni Cade Bambara, Angela Davis, and Muhammad Ali. At the same time, she was a frequent guest lecturer at Yale and other universities—and she wrote her own books.

Morrison began her first novel, *The Bluest Eye* (1970), while working with a writer's group. *Sula* (1973), *Song of Solomon* (1977), and *Tar Baby* (1981) followed. Helping to edit *The Black Book* (1974), an anthology of African American history, she encountered the true story of a runaway slave who killed her child so that she would not have to grow up in slavery. This idea developed into *Beloved* (1987), which became a Pulitzer Prize-winner. The author of seven novels, Morrison continues to receive wide acclaim. In 1993 she won the Nobel Prize for Literature.

Murasaki Shikibu (970s–1030?)

Novelist, diarist, poet

The few known details of Murasaki Shikibu's life come from a diary she kept for two years while in the service of the Empress Akiko. Even her real name is not recorded. She is called Lady Murasaki after the heroine of *Genji monogatari* (The tale of Genji), her monumental novel of life at the Japanese court.

Murasaki was exceptionally well educated. As a member of the Japanese nobility, she was expected to read and write her own language, but only boys learned Chinese, the language of government affairs. So she eavesdropped on her brother's Chinese lessons and was soon better at them than he was. Hearing this, her father exclaimed with pride but lamented that she was not a boy. She went on to marry, had one daughter, and became the empress' lady-in-waiting after her husband died in 1001.

Her *Tale of Genji*, which is considered the world's oldest novel, tells the story of the loves of the Emperor's son Genji, a charming hero whose name means "shining prince." Murasaki's poetic sensitivity, psychological insight, and beautiful descriptions of nature make it one of the greatest works of the imagination ever written.

Anna-Elisabeth de Noailles (1876–1933)

Poet, novelist, literary hostess

Of an aristocratic and exotic background—her mother was Greek and her father was a Romanian prince—Anna de Noailles was born in Paris and remained there for most of her life. She became a well-known literary figure, not just for her writing but for her wit and personality, which made her quite a popular salon hostess. Her many admirers included the poet Jean Cocteau and the novelist Colette.

Noailles's writing, with its sensual and romantic imagery, is reminiscent of 19th-century poetry. Natural themes and the cycles of life and death are prominent in her work. She is, however, quite literally, a 20th-century author, having published her first book, *Le coeur innombrable* (The numberless heart), in 1901.

Anna de Noailles died in Paris in 1933. Characteristically, her body was buried in one cemetery while her heart was buried in another, under a stone that reads, "Here sleeps my heart, witness to the wide world."

Marsha Norman (1947–)

Playwright

The playwright Marsha Norman is known for depicting the emotional pain and isolation of ordinary people, sensitively capturing their inner strength. She attributes much of this ability to her own lonely childhood in Louisville, Kentucky. As a girl, she read and wrote stories. Her most frequent companion was an imaginary friend she called Bettering. She left Kentucky for college but returned after graduation to work as a journalist, writing short children's pieces for Louisville papers. She also taught emotionally troubled teenagers at Kentucky Central State Hospital.

Impressed by Norman's work, John Jory, the director of the prominent Actors Theatre of Louisville, asked her to write a serious piece for his company. She reflected on her experience with the teenagers at the hospital and wrote her first play, *Getting Out*. After the Actors Theatre produced it in 1977, it did well in Los Angeles and New York.

Norman moved to New York in 1978 and wrote her most successful play, *'night Mother*. A chilling examination of suicide as revealed through the last conversation between a mother and daughter, it earned her the 1983 Pulitzer Prize. In 1991 she wrote the script for the successful Broadway musical *The Secret Garden*.

Joyce Carol Oates (1938–)

Novelist, short-story writer, essayist

Known for her dark, often violent explorations of evil, Joyce Carol Oates is one of the most acclaimed and most prolific writers of the day. Since her first volume of short stories, *By the North Gate*, appeared in 1963, she has published over 50 books—novels, short-story collections, and poetry.

Born in Millersport, New York, on the Erie Canal, Oates was the child of working-class parents. Before she could even read, she began inventing stories. She enjoyed her first literary success as a college student when her story, "In the Old World," won a *Mademoiselle* magazine fiction prize in 1959. While doing graduate work at the University of Wisconsin, she met her husband, Raymond J. Smith. The couple lived in Detroit for several years after 1962, and Oates has said that the social tension she witnessed there is one of her most profound inspirations.

Since 1978 Oates has taught creative writing at Princeton University in New Jersey. She also edits a literary journal, *The Ontario Review*, with her husband. Among the many honors she has received is the 1970 National Book Award for her novel *Them*.

Edna O'Brien (1930–)

Novelist, short-story writer, screenwriter

EDNA O'BRIEN'S WORK HAS AROUSED CONTROVERSY in her native Ireland, where some of her books have even been banned. Known for her candid, vivid descriptions and lyrical prose, she depicts the struggles, fleeting happinesses, and ultimate disillusionment of contemporary Irish women.

O'Brien began writing when she was still a student at a strict Catholic school. In the late 1950s, she moved with her husband and two children to London and dedicated herself to writing full-time. Her novels were successful from the first. *The Country Girls* (1960), spawned a trilogy that followed two women from their childhood in small-town Ireland to Dublin and finally to England. Other writings include the autobiographical *Mother Ireland* (1976), the story collection *A Scandalous Woman* (1974), and the novels *Night* (1972) and *Time and Tide* (1992). In all her works, O'Brien explores her Irish upbringing and feminist beliefs. Her critical attitude toward the Roman Catholic church has often brought her under fire in her home country.

O'Brien's career as a fiction writer has led to success in television and film writing as well. Still based in London, she often travels abroad as a lecturer.

Flannery O'Connor (1925–1964)

Novelist, short-story writer

FLANNERY O'CONNOR SPENT HER LAST MONTHS in a Georgia hospital, suffering from lupus, the same disease that killed her father. Even then, she continued to write the complex, haunting short stories collected in *Everything That Rises Must Converge* (1965) and published after her death at 39.

O'Connor was not a prolific writer, but her reputation was established early by two novels, *Wise Blood* (1952) and *The Violent Bear It Away* (1960), and a short-story collection, *A Good Man Is Hard to Find* (1955). As she expressed it, "my subject in fiction is the action of grace in territory held largely by the devil." Everything she wrote was informed by her Roman Catholicism. Her cast of characters, usually Southerners, are proud, willful oddballs, shocked into self-realization by violent encounters with strangers.

Born in Savannah, Georgia, O'Connor lived mostly on her mother's farm in Milledgeville. After graduating from Georgia College, she studied at the University of Iowa Writers' Workshop, publishing her first story in 1946. She enjoyed close friendships in the literary world, particularly with the poet Robert Lowell and the translator Robert Fitzgerald. She lived at the Fitzgeralds' Connecticut home for two years, until illness forced her to return to Georgia. O'Connor's active intelligence, religious faith, and wry sense of humor are tellingly shown in her letters, collected in *The Habit of Being* (1979).

Cynthia Ozick (1928–)

Novelist, essayist, translator

ALTHOUGH IT WAS FORBIDDEN FOR GIRLS TO ATTEND Hebrew school, five-year-old Cynthia Ozick's Russian immigrant parents insisted she go. The rabbi soon realized he had a brilliant pupil on his hands and encouraged Ozick's study of the religion that permeates her life and work. Growing up in the Bronx during the 1930s, Ozick attended high school in Manhattan and went to college at New York University before earning her master's degree from Ohio State University in 1951. Her first novel, *Trust*, appeared in 1966.

As a writer, Ozick strives to find a balance between her art and her faith. One of her most recurrent questions is whether the creative act violates the biblical commandment that forbids the making and worship of idols. In her stories she often uses magic and dream imagery, which are common devices in Hebrew texts.

Her works include the related stories, "The Shawl" and "Rosa" (published together in 1989) and *The Puttermesser Papers* (1997), a collection of tales about one of her favorite characters, Ruth Puttermesser. The winner of many awards, and the author of essays as well as translations from Yiddish, Ozick is an established voice in the Jewish-American community.

Grace Paley (1922–)

Short-story writer

THROUGH HER POWER OF OBSERVATION AND passion for politics, Grace Paley has carved a place for herself in the world of short fiction. Born to Russian political exiles in New York City, she attended Hunter College and New York University, but eventually left to pursue poetry. She married Jess Paley and, before separating, the couple had two children. Working as a typist to support her children, she wrote whenever possible. In 1959 she published her first short-story collection, *The Little Disturbances of Man: Stories of Men and Women in Love.*

Acclaimed for its accurate depiction of urban Jewish life, *Little Disturbances* helped launch Paley's teaching career. Her interest in political activism increased, and Paley protested conditions in New York prisons and the Vietnam War. She attended the World Peace Conference in 1973 and continued to teach and write, publishing her second collection of short stories, *Enormous Changes at the Last Minute*, a year later. Again her stories examined urban existence—and reflected her political values. She continues to be an active teacher, writer, and crusader for world peace.

Dorothy Parker (1893–1967)

Short-story writer, critic, screenwriter

DOROTHY PARKER'S OUTRAGEOUSLY WITTY REMARKS lit up New York during the Roaring Twenties. She once described an actress as having a range that ran "the gamut of emotions from A to B."

Parker worked as a theater and book reviewer for such magazines as *Vanity Fair* and *The New Yorker*. Her light verse was, and still is, widely quoted. Her stories, collected in *Laments for the Living* (1930), *After Such Pleasures* (1933), and *Here Lies* (1939), demonstrate her gift for dialogue. That talent served her well as a screenwriter in Hollywood. Mostly, though, Parker lived in New York City. She and her image were inseparable from it.

Like many talented comics, Parker's life was anything but funny. She endured difficult marriages, failed affairs, alcoholism, and writer's block; she tried to commit suicide twice. But her stories of women trapped in the game of trying to please men are memorable, funny, and sad. The story "Big Blonde" won the O. Henry Prize for 1929. "A tough quotable female humorist," as she described herself, Parker dissected the deadness at the core of the "smart" society life.

Christine de Pisan (1364–1430?)

Poet, historian

THE DAUGHTER OF A VENETIAN COURT PHYSICIAN, Christine de Pisan grew up in France after her father was hired as the astrologer to the French King Charles V. She was educated by her father and learned Italian, French, and Latin. At age 15, she married Étienne du Castel, a 25-year-old court secretary. Their happy marriage ended only ten years later, when her husband died in an epidemic, leaving her with three children. To support them, she began the writing career for which she has lately been recognized.

Christine's earliest works were lyrical poems, written according to the established conventions of courtly love. Gradually, she introduced personal, political, and moral themes into her ballads and lovers' laments. Popular at court, she attracted powerful patrons. Next, she turned to prose. In 1404 she wrote a biography of Charles V. Rejecting the way the well-known 13th-century ballad "The Romance of the Rose" belittled women, she wrote "Letter from the God of Loves," the first of many feminist works. Her *Book of the City of Ladies* (1405) profiled virtuous women of courage.

Throughout Christine's life, France was in the grips of the Hundred Years' War with England, and it is believed that she retired to a Dominican convent around 1418. No later writings of hers exist until 1429, when she wrote joyfully of the victorious Joan of Arc.

Sylvia Plath (1932–1963)

Poet, novelist

SYLVIA PLATH'S NOVEL, *THE BELL JAR*, TELLS THE story of her own breakdown and attempted suicide while she was at college. It appeared in 1963, two weeks before she killed herself by inhaling gas from an oven. She was not yet a well-known poet, and the drama of her death still sometimes overshadows the accomplishment of her hallucinatory, intensely personal verse.

Plath grew up in Massachusetts and was devoted to her German father, who died when she was eight. A brilliant student, she attended Smith College on scholarship, won a guest editor's slot at *Mademoiselle* magazine her junior year, and graduated *summa cum laude* (with highest honors). Plagued by insecurities, however, Plath was torn between her compulsive desire to succeed as an artist and her need to appear all-American and wholesome.

While on a Fulbright Fellowship to England in 1956, Plath married the poet Ted Hughes. They dreamed of creating a literary partnership, but Plath put Hughes first, typing manuscripts and promoting his work. Her book of poems, *The Colossus*, was not published until 1960, the year her daughter was born. A son followed in 1962, and shortly afterward she learned Hughes had been unfaithful. During her last months of life, as she struggled with alternating depression and hopefulness, her creativity exploded. The poems that would make up *Ariel* (1965) poured forth wholly formed, passionate and redemptive. Her *Collected Poems* (1981) was awarded a posthumous Pulitzer Prize in 1982.

Dawn Powell (1897–1965)

Novelist

ALTHOUGH DAWN POWELL'S WORK WAS RECEIVED enthusiastically by other writers, it was never popular, perhaps simply because she didn't write the way a woman was expected to. All 16 of her novels went out of print soon after her death. Then in 1987, Powell's friend, the writer Gore Vidal, published an essay about her that has helped bring her novels the attention they deserve.

Born in Ohio, Powell lived with many different

relatives around the Midwest after her mother's death. After graduating from Lake Erie College in 1918, she moved to New York City and remained there for the rest of her life.

Powell's novels are about the places she knew best, the Midwest and Greenwich Village in New York, and they offer a profound but comic portrait of middle-class society. In *Angels on Toast* (1940), two of the main characters have come on a business trip from Chicago to New York. Her last work, *The Golden Spur* (1962), takes place when the New York of Powell's youth is beginning to be torn down. She died in relative obscurity soon after it was published.

Ann Radcliffe (1764–1823)

Gothic novelist

ANN RADCLIFFE, ONE OF THE BEST-KNOWN English Gothic novelists, was raised in London and Bath in comfortable surroundings. She married William Radcliffe in 1788 and soon settled in London. William began a career as a journalist and encouraged his wife to write, too.

Her first novel was not a particular success, but the next, *A Sicilian Romance* (1790), was instantly popular. The public response to her most famous novel, *The Mysteries of Udolpho* (1794), was so enthusiastic that the Radcliffes embarked on a tour of continental Europe to escape the excessive attention of their fans.

Ann's career was in full swing when she stopped publishing at age 33. Rumors flew that she was ill, even that she had suffered a mysterious fate worthy of one of her novels. More reasonable guesses included speculation that she had become too wealthy to need to write, or that she was appalled by the poor imitations her novels had inspired. Ann and her husband traveled happily for years before she died at age 60. A novel and a poem written after her retirement were published posthumously by her husband.

Adrienne Rich (1929–)

Poet, feminist, activist

ADRIENNE RICH'S FATHER, A DOCTOR, ENDORSED her early interest in poetry, while her artistically gifted mother left a musical career to raise her two daughters. Rich graduated from Radcliffe College in 1951, the year *A Change of World*, her first book, was published. At first she kept to traditional poetic forms, a choice that mirrored her conservative, middle-class upbringing. She married and had three sons. As the 1960s progressed, though, she became increasingly engaged by the women's movement. She turned to activism, and her writings evolved accordingly, as she searched for new expressions, new definitions of what it means to be a woman. Political protest and questions of sexuality found their way into her work. Rich sounded an alarm with her poetic insights, urging women to resist the traditional patriarchal domination of myth, language, and history.

The importance of Rich's contribution to American poetry cannot be overstated. Without sacrificing grace or craft, she condemns violence, racism, and homophobia, seeking to establish new literary traditions for women, and rediscover women's history.

When Rich won a National Book Award for her collection, *Diving into the Wreck* (1973), she accepted the honor in the name of all women who have been stripped of their voices. Her poetry books include

Snapshots of a Daughter-in-Law (1963) and *An Atlas of the Difficult World* (1991). Her essays, collected in such volumes as *Blood, Bread, and Poetry* (1986), are widely read, and her book-length prose work, *Of Woman Born* (1976), is a landmark study of motherhood.

Christina Georgina Rossetti (1830–1894)

Poet

CHRISTINA ROSSETTI BELONGED TO AN ARTISTIC family. Her Italian father, exiled in England for his political activities, was a musician and poet. Her mother wrote a study of the Italian poet Dante. And her brother, Dante Gabriel Rossetti, was a leading figure in the Pre-Raphaelite Brotherhood of painters and writers inspired by the Italian Renaissance. Rossetti herself became the most important woman poet of her day.

The family's financial troubles and her own ill health kept Rossetti for the most part close to home. For over 30 years, she lived with and cared for her father and then her mother, constant to her religious devotions and poetry. Her first work, *Verses* (1847), was published privately by her grandfather Gaetano Polidori when she was 17. Several of her poems appeared under a pseudonym in the Pre-Raphaelite magazine, *The Germ*. *Goblin Market and Other Poems* (1862), a fantastical allegory of temptation and renunciation, established her fame. A delicate beauty, Rossetti often served as a model for the Pre-Raphaelite painters. She was courted by two men whom she loved but rejected because of religious differences.

Rossetti died of cancer at the age of 64. Among the works that contributed to her reputation were *The Prince's Progress and Other Poems* (1866), *Commonplace and Other Short Stories* (1870), and the popular Victorian children's book *Sing-Song: A Nursery Rhyme Book* (1872).

Muriel Rukeyser (1913–1980)

Poet, biographer, critic, novelist, translator, activist

MURIEL RUKEYSER HAD A SHELTERED CHILDHOOD in New York City, something she realized while still a schoolgirl: A teacher once asked if any-one in the class was familiar with any streets other than those that led from their homes to school. Rukeyser didn't.

After that, Rukeyser began to seek life's pleasures and perils. By the time she was 20, she had plunged into a life of political activism. She attended the Scottsboro trials, in which nine black men were accused of rape in Alabama, and investigated dangerous working conditions for miners in West Virginia. Married briefly in 1945, she chose to have a child on her own a few years later. In the 1970s, she traveled to Hanoi to protest the Vietnam War and was arrested for antiwar actions in the United States.

Always, she expressed faith in humanity's possibilities and outrage at injustice. She shaped her personal and political experiences into colloquial, moving poems, many of which are in *The Collected Poems of Muriel Rukeyser* (1978). She also published biographies, plays, criticism, and translations. Rukeyser's work has never been as widely read as she deserves. Many critics consider her a major poetic voice of her time.

Nelly Sachs (1891–1970)

Poet, dramatist

AWARDED THE NOBEL PRIZE FOR LITERATURE IN 1966, Nelly Sachs is regarded as the leading poet of the Holocaust. It is true that much of her work addresses Nazi persecution and eulogizes the Jewish people. But many themes in her work—birth, faith, life, love, renewal—are universal.

The child of Jewish parents, Sachs grew up in Berlin. Wealthy, nonreligious, and cultured, she painted and wrote plays and poetry, but none of these very seriously. Her young life seemed only to be troubled by an unhappy love affair and the growing threat of the Nazis. In 1940 Sachs and her mother escaped from Germany, just hours before they were scheduled to be deported to a labor camp. They settled in Stockholm, Sweden. Sachs, an admirer of Selma Lagerlöf, had corresponded with the Swedish writer for years, and Lagerlöf had obtained permission for the emigration.

Sachs's writings became urgent, impassioned. She often used a language of coded meanings, with themes and imagery recalling biblical writing. Dedicating her first volume of poetry, *In den Wohnungen des Todes* (1946, In the habitations of death), to the Jews who died at Auschwitz, she recreated the horrors of the death camp. Her later works include the verse play *Eli* (1951) and the poetry collection *Noch feiert Tod das Leben* (1961, Death still celebrates life).

George Sand (1804–1876)

French novelist, feminist

IN HER FIRST NOVEL, *INDIANA* (1832), GEORGE Sand rejects the restrictions placed upon women in marriage and defends a woman who leaves her husband for romantic love. Like most of her work, it was based on her life, and it was immediately popular. Her prolific writings include novels, essays, an autobiography, and nearly 20,000 letters. A political activist during the French Republican Revolution of 1848, Sand supported women's education and equality between the sexes.

Amandine-Aurore-Lucille Dupin was born to a mother of humble origin and an aristocratic father. After her father's death when she was four, Amandine was raised by her paternal grandmother on the family estate at Nohant. She married the Baron Dudevant when she was 18 and had two children but left him in 1831. Moving to Paris, she began her brilliant career as a writer, taking the pseudonym George Sand. She became notorious as a lover to famous men, especially the poet Alfred de Musset and the composer Frédéric Chopin. An eccentric, she shocked many with her masculine dress, cigar-smoking, and free behavior.

Among Sand's best novels are *Mauprat* (1837) and *Consuelo* (1842). Her later works, known as the "rustic novels" because they were about the country peasants she knew as a girl, are considered some of the most beautiful works of their kind.

Sappho (late 7th–mid-8th century B.C.E.)

Poet

NINE VOLUMES OF SAPPHO'S POETRY WERE collected in the third and second centuries B.C.E. She was admired during her lifetime and for centuries after, and was praised by ancient scholars

such as Aristotle, Horace, and Ovid. Today only fragments of her work remain—two poems, at most, are considered to be complete. Most of her writings were destroyed, or simply not preserved, by medieval scribes. Nevertheless, she is still considered one of the greatest poets of ancient Greece, and modern poets continue to be influenced by her lyrical stanzas.

Sappho was born on Lesbos, an island off Turkey. Little else is certain about her. She may have belonged to an aristocratic family of wine merchants, married, and had a daughter. She seems to have been exiled to Sicily for a time. It is known that hers was a cultured society where women were accepted in male company and educated. Sappho composed music and love poems to men and women alike. Because of the fervor of her poems addressed to women, she is considered the muse of lesbian lovers. Even the brief fragments of her work that have survived attest to her genius for capturing the sensations of love: "As a whirlwind/swoops on an oak/Love shakes my heart."

Sei Shonagon (approximately 966–1013)

Diarist

Sei Shonagon, the daughter of a poet, served as a lady-in-waiting in the court of Empress Sadako in Japan. She was not noted for her beauty, but her brilliant wit ensured her a following. During her decade at court, she recorded observations and thoughts in a diary, *Makura no soshi* (The pillow book). She organized her impressions by classifying them into subjects such as "annoying things," or "things which distract in moments of boredom." Then she listed whatever events, people, or objects fell into that category, including even such vivid details as smells.

The Pillow Book stands apart from the diary of the other, more serious, writer from the same period, Murasaki Shikubu. Sei Shonagon is known for her biting humor and frequently merciless teasing. She apparently made quite a few enemies. Little is known about her life after she left the royal household. It is believed that she spent her last years in troubled solitude. Today, Sei Shonagon's writings offer invaluable insight into the daily intrigues and details of the tenth-century Japanese royal court.

Marie de Rabutin-Chantal, Marquise de Sévigné (1626–1696)

Letter writer

Marie de Rabutin-Chantal, born into a noble Parisian family, was raised by an uncle after the deaths of her parents and, some years later, of her grandparents. Life in her uncle's household was happy, and Marie received an excellent education. In 1644 she married Henri Marquis de Sévigné, a suitably noble but reckless young man. He died in a duel in 1651, leaving her with a son and a daughter.

Madame de Sévigné settled in Paris where she frequented the most fashionable salons and became a member of the court of King Louis XIV. The witty, beautiful widow attracted many suitors, but she preferred to remain independent. She dedicated her energies to her children, particularly her daughter, Françoise-Marguerite.

> **"I am going to tell you a thing the most astonishing, the most surprising, the most marvelous, the most miraculous, the most magnificent, the most confounding, the most unheard of, the most singular, the most extraordinary, the most incredible, the most unforeseen, the greatest, the least, the rarest, the most common, the most public, the most private till today, the most brilliant, the most enviable . . . a thing that we cannot believe at Paris; how then will it gain credit at Lyon?"**
>
> **Letter from the MARQUISE DE SÉVIGNÉ to her cousin, telling him of a wedding engagement**

After Françoise-Marguerite married, she moved to Provence, and Marie wrote to her daily to give her the news of Paris. These letters provide an entertaining account of Madame de Sévigné's life: gossip, current events, and philosophical musings are all expressed with extraordinary style. Thirty years after Madame de Sévigné's death, her granddaughter recognized their literary value and published them. Afterward, letters she had written to other correspondents were made public as well, bringing the total to nearly 3,000.

Anne Sexton (1928–1974)

Poet

IN 1955, FOLLOWING THE BIRTH OF HER SECOND daughter, Anne Sexton suffered such a severe breakdown that she had to be hospitalized. Her psychiatrist suggested writing poetry as an outlet for her depression. From her very first attempts, she received positive recognition. Sexton was admitted to poetry workshops taught by the well-known poets W. D. Snodgrass and Robert Lowell, and she became friends with many writers, especially poet Maxine Kumin. Critics praised her first collection, *To Bedlam and Part Way Back* (1960), which centered around her experiences in the mental hospital.

Sexton's poetry focuses on her personal, interior life; she was not an academic. The daughter of a wool merchant, she grew up in Wellesley, Massachusetts, and eloped with Alfred ("Kayo") Sexton instead of going to college. Once she began writing, Sexton published poetry at an astonishing rate, and taught at several universities.

Sexton routinely received wonderful reviews and prestigious awards, including a Pulitzer Prize for *Live or Die* (1966) and a Guggenheim fellowship in 1969. Nevertheless, she could not shake her profound unhappiness. Her public persona was glamorous and confident, but in private, her fears and anxieties tortured her. In 1974, after a 20-year-long struggle with depression, Anne Sexton committed suicide. She remains one of the most celebrated American women poets of the century.

Ntozake Shange (1948–)

Playwright, poet, novelist, performer

NTOZAKE SHANGE'S "CHOREOPOEM," *FOR COLORED girls who have considered suicide/when the rainbow is enuf*, made its Off-Broadway debut in 1976 and received enthusiastic critical acclaim. The piece documents seven black women's experiences using traditional methods such as music, dance, storytelling, and poetry. The women relive difficult times, but they end the play positively, united in a moment of self-awareness.

Although Shange writes about oppression, she focuses on survivors rather than victims, drawing on myths and traditions of strength. Considering language itself to be a means of protest, she has devised her own way of using it, often writing in all lowercase letters, spelling words phonetically, and putting slashes at the ends of her sentences instead of periods.

She was born Paulette Williams and experienced a privileged childhood. Her parents were friends with prominent African American artists, musicians, and intellectuals and often took their children abroad. Paulette did not feel the effects of racism until they moved away from the East Coast and she attended a newly integrated school in St. Louis, Missouri.

In 1971 she changed her name legally, choosing the Zulu words *Ntozake*, which means "she who comes with her own things," and *Shange*, "she who walks like a lion." Shange has also published volumes of poetry, one of which is *Nappy Edges* (1978), and novels such as *Betsey Brown* (1985).

Leslie Marmon Silko (1948–)

Novelist, poet

LESLIE MARMON SILKO IS ONE OF THE MOST acclaimed Native American writers to emerge in the last 25 years. She is best known for her novel *Ceremony* (1977) and its follow-up, *Almanac of the Dead* (1991), as well as her anthology of autobiographical poetry and prose, *Storyteller* (1981).

Raised on the Laguna Pueblo Reservation near Albuquerque, New Mexico, Silko comes from a mixed heritage of Laguna, Mexican, and Anglo-American backgrounds. She attended grade school at the reservation and participated in many Pueblo ceremonies, although not in the same ways that a full-blooded Pueblo would have been allowed. As a child, Silko was told many stories, true and legendary, by her Native American and white relatives. The importance of preserving oral traditions would become a major theme in her writings.

In 1969 Silko graduated *summa cum laude* (with high honors) from the University of New Mexico and began to study law, intending to focus on Native American issues. She soon decided that she could address many of the same concerns by becoming a writer and teacher instead. The recipient of many honors, in 1981 she received a prestigious MacArthur Foundation Fellowship, which allowed her to devote herself to creative projects for several years. She lives and works in Tucson, Arizona.

Kate Simon (1912–1990)

Travel writer, memoirist

KATE SIMON'S FIRST JOURNEY WASN'T UNDERTAKEN for pleasure, but she later credited it with sparking her career as a travel writer. When she was four, Simon emigrated with her mother and brother from poverty-stricken Warsaw, Poland, to America. While her mother arranged the trip, little Kate took care of her brother, and she remembered that responsibility—the way she paid attention to every detail—for the rest of her life.

The travelers settled in the Bronx, New York, and Simon went on to attend Hunter College, work as a secretary, and write book reviews for magazines. Then she wrote a guidebook to the city's inexpensive but great restaurants. The success of *New York Places and Pleasures: An Uncommon Guidebook* (1959) led to similar guides for Mexico, England, and Italy. Simon was particularly praised for her engaging style and her attention to lesser-known places. In the 1980s Simon wrote two acclaimed autobiographies, *Bronx Primitive* (1982) and *A Wider World* (1986), vividly evoking the New York immigrant community of her youth.

Dame Edith Sitwell (1887–1964)

Poet, critic

RAISED IN A WEALTHY, ENGLISH LITERARY FAMILY, Edith Sitwell proclaimed when she was a young girl that she intended to become a "genius." Her first collection, *The Mother and Other Poems* (1915), was filled with romantic and exotic imagery. She was accused by some critics of using contrived language, but the purposefully artificial world she created appealed to others. By the early 1920s, Sitwell and her two writer brothers, Osbert and Sacheverell, had

become a popular literary trio, attracting the attention of such writers as Virginia Woolf and T. S. Eliot.

In 1930 Sitwell entered into her second phase of poetry, trading her dreamy mood poems for those that examined and criticized modern society. Typical of this period, *Five Variations on a Theme* (1933) was honored with a medal by the Royal Society of Literature. In her final literary period, Sitwell turned her attention to the spiritual rather than the earthly, becoming a Roman Catholic in 1942.

A true eccentric, Sitwell wore Elizabethan clothes and expressed her opinions with vigor. Her relationships—both friendships and rivalries—were always lively and interesting. In addition to poetry, she also published literary criticism, biography, and autobiography.

Susan Sontag (1933–)

Novelist, essayist, intellectual

Susan Sontag was always an ambitious student. When teachers at her Los Angeles high school assigned reading from *Reader's Digest*, she sought out far more sophisticated essays from the *Partisan Review.* After attending college at the University of Chicago, she went on to earn two master's degrees from Harvard University and studied at the University of Paris. Sontag then joined academia herself and taught philosophy at universities in the New York City area. At the same time, she contributed articles to many journals, among them her old favorite, *Partisan Review*, and *Commentary*. Sontag published her first novel, *The Benefactor*, in 1963. While she received critical acclaim for the book, her real breakthrough came with the publication of her essay on cultural aesthetics, "Notes on 'Camp'" (1964).

Sontag's essays and philosophical observations have been collected in several books, including *Against Interpretation* (1966) and *On Photography* (1977). She is renowned for her explorations of contemporary culture. Sontag has also considered the way modern society perceives and reacts to sickness in her books *Illness as Metaphor* (1978), written after she was diagnosed with breast cancer, and in *AIDS and Its Metaphors* (1989).

Germaine de Staël (1766–1817)

Writer, political essayist, literary hostess

Madame Germaine de Staël is remembered chiefly for her influence on literary criticism and political theory. Her father, Jacques Necker, a Swiss banker, was finance minister to the French King

Louis XVI; her mother, Suzanne Necker, was a famed beauty and literary hostess. After marrying the Swedish ambassador, Baron Erik de Staël-Holstein, Germaine established herself at the center of her own intellectual circle.

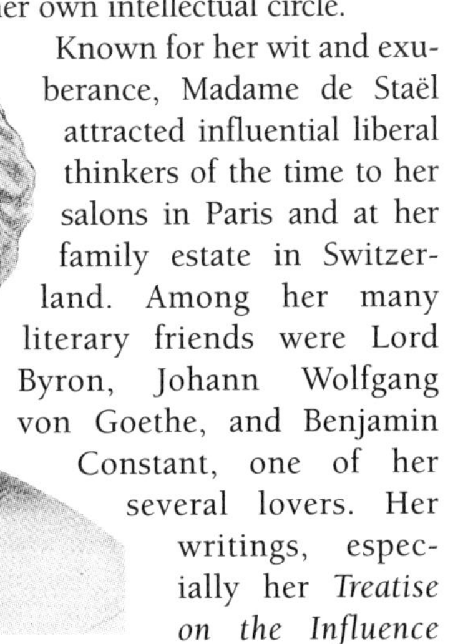

Known for her wit and exuberance, Madame de Staël attracted influential liberal thinkers of the time to her salons in Paris and at her family estate in Switzerland. Among her many literary friends were Lord Byron, Johann Wolfgang von Goethe, and Benjamin Constant, one of her several lovers. Her writings, especially her *Treatise on the Influence of the Passions upon the Happiness of Individuals and Nations* (1796), made significant contributions to the Romantic movement in literature and to revolutionary politics.

Originally a supporter of the French Revolution, Madame de Staël always opposed tyranny. Her defense of individual liberty provided a ray of light during the Reign of Terror in France. She made no secret of her disapproval of Napoleon's growing despotism and spent a decade in exile as a result.

Madame de Staël remains a vital literary presence. Her fiction is less celebrated than her critical and historical writings. Nevertheless, her novels, *Delphine* (1802) and *Corinne* (1807), with their accounts of talented, spirited, and unconventional women, continue to interest readers.

Freya Madeleine Stark (1893–1993)

Travel writer, letter writer

FREYA STARK'S BOHEMIAN CHILDHOOD, MARKED BY frequent travel, laid the groundwork for the independent, adventurous adult she was to become. The daughter of English artists, Stark lived in Italy with her mother and sister after she was eight. Provided with little formal education, she learned French and German on her own. She enrolled at London University in 1912.

Stark worked as a nurse in Italy during World War I but eventually returned to the university to specialize in Oriental Studies. She then made her first journey to the Middle East, visiting Jerusalem, Lebanon, and Cairo in 1927. The correspondence from this trip was collected and published as *Letters from Syria* (1942). Stark went on to explore places that few Europeans, particularly women, dared to visit. Her dashing travel books were enthusiastically received, particularly *The Valley of the Assassins* (1934), an account of her journeys in Persia (modern-day Iran).

During World War II, Stark worked in Baghdad, Iraq; the Yemenite city of Aden; and Cairo, Egypt, to counteract enemy propaganda and promote the British cause. She continued to produce countless letters and sketches. Her insightful, entertaining accounts of faraway lands, combined with bits of travel advice, assured her popularity. Active well into her 80s, Stark died at her home in Asolo, Italy, three months after her 100th birthday.

Christina Ellen Stead (1902–1983)

Novelist, short-story writer

BORN IN ROCKDALE, SYDNEY, AUSTRALIA, CHRISTINA Stead was only two years old when her mother died. Her father remarried and eventually had six more children, so Stead grew up the oldest sister in a bustling family. After college, she worked as a teacher before leaving Australia in 1928 for a life of travel. In London she met her future husband, the American writer William Blake. They went on to live in Paris and the United States, where she taught at New York University and spent several years in Hollywood. Then the couple returned to Europe. Blake died in 1968, and Stead went home to Australia six years later, remaining there until her death.

Christina Stead's writings were praised by critics, particularly for their portrayals of women struggling against the roles imposed upon them by society. Her masterpiece is the novel *The Man Who Loved Children* (1940), for which she adapted some circumstances of her own childhood: a large family presided over by an egotistical father. Other novels include *The House of All Nations* (1938) and *For Love Alone* (1944). Stead also wrote short stories and translated literary works from French.

Gertrude Stein (1874–1946)

Poet, playwright, critic

Gertrude Stein possessed brilliant literary talent but wrote in an experimental style that has stymied readers, enraging some but delighting others. The youngest of seven children born to wealthy parents, Stein was orphaned in her teens. She studied philosophy and psychology at Radcliffe College and attended Johns Hopkins Medical School for four years. But she lost interest in becoming a doctor. Instead, she set up a salon in Paris with her brother Leo, and they welcomed the most illustrious artists of the day. Inspired by the cubist style being used by painters she knew, Stein adapted the idea for her writing, making use of repetition, fragmented reality, and obscured meaning, and trying to capture a sense of movement in the language itself. Pablo Picasso painted a famous portrait of her, and she wrote several pieces about him.

Her companion for life was Alice B. Toklas, whom she met when Toklas visited Paris in 1907. Toklas typed Stein's manuscripts, helped edit them, and, after Stein's death, arranged for the publication of many unpublished pieces. During the 1920s and 1930s, their apartment at 27 rue des Fleurus was a mecca for American expatriate writers such as Ernest Hemingway and F. Scott Fitzgerald.

Stein's writings, which can be as difficult to categorize as to comprehend, are many and varied. They include the novella collection *Three Lives* (1909); her book of poetry composed in the manner of abstract paintings, *Tender Buttons* (1914); and the opera *Four Saints in Three Acts* (1934). *The Autobiography of Alice B. Toklas* (1933), in spite of its name, is really her own memoir.

A SHAWL

"A shawl is a hat and hurt and a red ballon and an under coat and a sizer a sizer of talks.

A shawl is a wedding, a piece of wax a little build. A shawl.

Pick a ticket, pick it in strange steps and with hollows. There is hollow hollow belt, a belt is a shawl."

Gertrude Stein
Tender Buttons

Alfonsina Storni (1892–1938)

Poet

As a young girl in San Juan, Argentina, Alfonsina Storni helped her mother support the family by doing needlework. At age 14, she joined a touring theater troupe as an actress and traveled around Argentina before settling down to earn her teaching certificate. She got a job at a country school, but fell in love with a married man and fled to Buenos Aires to protect his identity when she gave birth to their son.

In the city Storni taught and worked as a director at a children's theater. She began to write poetry on the side and joined the literary scene. Her first volume of poetry, *La inquietud del rosal* (1916, The restless rose garden), used intense, often aggressive, language to express her feminist beliefs. As her poetry evolved, however, her central theme changed from questioning society and the traditional roles of men and women to a more reflective phase. The poems in *Mundo de siete pozos* (1934, World of seven walls) examine the deep inner world that attracted Storni during this time.

In 1938 Alfonsina Storni committed suicide, fearing that the cancer she had had surgery for three years earlier had spread to her lungs. She is remembered as one of Argentina's outstanding female poets.

Harriet Beecher Stowe (1811–1896)

Novelist, essayist

"SO THIS IS THE LITTLE LADY WHO STARTED THE big war," Abraham Lincoln said to Harriet Beecher Stowe when they met in 1862. A decade earlier Stowe's novel *Uncle Tom's Cabin* had taken America by storm, selling 300,000 copies in its first year.

Born in Connecticut to the famous Beecher family, Harriet grew up surrounded by Protestant ministers—her father and seven brothers all chose the same path. The family moved to Cincinnati, Ohio, in 1832. There she met runaway slaves who crossed the border from Kentucky and welcomed black children to her Sunday school classes. In 1836 she married the religious scholar Calvin Stowe.

Harriet found married life difficult. Cold and odd, Calvin could not support his wife and seven

children. She struggled with depression and poverty, particularly after they moved to Maine. A vision she had of a slave's death by beating inspired *Uncle Tom's Cabin*. The book not only ended her financial worries, it also had an extremely positive effect on the abolition movement. In response to violent criticism from pro-slavery groups, she published *The Key to Uncle Tom* (1853), which contained writings by former slaves.

But Harriet Stowe wasn't a one-story phenomenon. She went on to write evocatively about New England life. In addition to such novels as *The Minister's Wooing* (1859) and *The Pearl of Orr's Island* (1862), she was the author of articles, stories, and poems.

Amy Tan (1952–)

Novelist, short-story writer

AS A CHILD AMY TAN DESPERATELY WANTED TO be like her schoolmates in California, but her traditional Chinese parents had very different expectations. The tension was especially strong between the girl and her mother. Sorrow struck the family—Tan's father and older brother both died of brain tumors—and they moved to Switzerland. Her mother's increased dependence and higher expectations only made Tan rebel more strongly. The situation became nearly intolerable, but then Tan learned about her mother's early life in China, and a newfound respect was born. Mother-daughter relationships and the interaction between cultures have become central themes in all Tan's fiction.

Tan turned to fiction after establishing a career as a freelance business writer. Her first novel, *The Joy Luck Club*, was published in 1989. The book follows seven women—three Chinese mothers and four Chinese-American daughters—as they struggle to understand one another. It was a success, and Tan went on to write the screenplay for a popular film adaptation.

Tan's second novel, *The Kitchen God's Wife* (1991), directly addresses her mother's own tragic experiences. In it, a mother tells her American-born daughter about the hardships she endured in war-torn China. Tan has also published two children's stories about Chinese-American experiences and traditions.

Ida Minerva Tarbell (1857–1944)

Journalist, historian

IDA TARBELL WAS RAISED IN PENNSYLVANIA BY progressive parents who encouraged her academic interests. After earning a college degree in biology and finding few opportunities for women scientists, Tarbell turned to history and journalism. She began publishing serial biographies of historical figures such as Abraham Lincoln and Napoleon Bonaparte in *McClure's* magazine.

When *McClure's* assigned her to investigate John D. Rockefeller's Standard Oil Company, Tarbell embarked on the project that would establish her as a "muckraking" journalist—seeking to reveal corruption through her findings. Her groundbreaking exposé, *The History of the Standard Oil Company*, was published in installments between 1901 and 1904. In

it she denounced the "reptilian principle of special privilege," which she considered dangerous to the ideal of equal opportunity. Rockefeller tried to dismiss her, calling her "Miss Tarbarrel," but the articles prompted federal investigations. As a result, the Standard Oil monopoly was broken up in 1911 under the Sherman Anti-Trust Act.

Tarbell went on to write other exhaustively researched biographies and exposés. *The Tariff in Our Time* (1911) revealed how taxes on imports and exports enriched special interests at the expense of workers and consumers. She never married; her dedication to her career was too complete. Puzzlingly, although Tarbell lived like a feminist, she did not support women's suffrage. She believed that women's moral influence would be diluted by involvement in public life.

Teresa of Ávila (1515–1582)

Mystic, writer

THE FIRST SIGN OF TERESA DE CEPEDA Y Ahumada's spiritual enthusiasm came when the seven-year-old girl and her brother ran away from home, planning to die as martyrs and meet God. Fortunately, their uncle met them on the road and brought them back.

Teresa had a happy girlhood in Ávila, Spain, and enjoyed reading chivalric romances. But, in 1529, her mother died, and she turned again to religion. Eventually, she became a nun in the local Carmelite order, a group founded by Christian pilgrims who had originally settled on Mount Carmel in Palestine. She was 39 when she had a vision of Jesus, the first of the several mystical experiences that she describes in her autobiography.

In 1558 Teresa began working to restore the Carmelites order to austerity, poverty, and chastity, commitments that had vanished during the preceding century. She traveled widely, founding convents. At her encouragement, a priest called Saint John of the Cross initiated the same reforms for Carmelite monks.

Her writings, which include *The Way of Perfection* (1583) and *The Interior Castle* (1588), are masterpieces of religious literature. She was officially declared a saint in 1622 and later became the patron saint of Spain.

Barbara Wertheim Tuchman (1912–1989)

Historian

BARBARA WERTHEIM WAS BORN IN NEW YORK City into a prestigious banking family. After graduating from Radcliffe College in 1933, she spent a year in Tokyo working for the Institute of Pacific

> **"Books are the carriers of civilization. Without books, history is silent, literature dumb, science crippled, thought and speculation at a standstill. Without books, the development of civilization would have been impossible. They are engines of change, windows on the world . . . They are companions, teachers, magicians, bankers of the treasures of the mind. Books are humanity in print."**
>
> **BARBARA TUCHMAN**
> ***Authors League Bulletin*, 1979**

Relations. Then she took a staff job at the magazine *The Nation,* covering stories from the Spanish Civil War to international politics.

Marriage to the physician Lester Tuchman brought her career as a journalist to a close. For several years, she devoted herself to their three children. Eventually, though, Tuchman returned to the historical research she had always loved and began writing books. In 1963 she won the Pulitzer Prize for *The Guns of August*, in which she recounted the first weeks of World War I. She was awarded a second Pulitzer Prize for her work on *Stilwell and the American Experience in China, 1911–45* (1970).

In 1978 Tuchman published a best-seller, *A Distant Mirror: The Calamitous 14th Century.* The next year she became the first woman president of the American Academy and Institute of Arts and Letters, an organization established to honor outstanding American artists and literary figures. Noted for her gripping narrative style, Tuchman made intricate historical events not only accessible but compelling to the general public.

Sigrid Undset (1882–1949)

Novelist, short-story writer, memoirist

SIGRID UNDSET'S CHILDHOOD WAS MARKED BY her father's illness. Too weak to read himself, Ingvald Undset, a famous archaeologist, often had his young daughter read aloud from medieval Scandinavian literature. Norwegian history and folklore would prove to be a lifelong passion for her.

Undset's first attempt at writing, a novel about medieval Norway, didn't interest publishers, so she produced *Fru Marta Oulie* (1907, Mrs. Marta Oulie), the story of a modern career woman like herself—she had spent ten years working in an office. Eventually, though, she returned to historical settings.

Based in medieval times and spanning three volumes, *Kristin Lavransdatter* (1920–1922) chronicled the life of the title character. The four-volume *Olaf Audunsson i Hestviken* (1925–1927, The master of Hestviken) was also set in medieval Scandinavia. In both series, the principal characters experience a growing devotion to God, which reflected the spiritual course of Undset's own life; she became a Roman Catholic in 1925. The novels earned her the 1928 Nobel Prize.

Undset, an early and outspoken critic of the Nazi regime, was forced to spend the war years in the United States. In later life, she wrote autobiographical works as well as fiction. These include *Elleve aar* (1934, Eleven years) and *Happy Times in Norway* (1942).

Uno Chiyo (1897–1996)

Novelist, short-story writer, editor

VERSATILE, FLAMBOYANT UNO CHIYO WAS FAMOUS for scandalously defying Japanese tradition in her youth. Ultimately, however, she built a reputation for producing serious literary work. In 1990, after a career that spanned nearly 70 years, she was named "a person of cultural merit" by the Japanese emperor.

Uno began her first job, as a teaching assistant, in 1914. There, she astounded her coworkers, not only by wearing makeup, but because she had an affair with another teacher. She was soon fired. Moving to Tokyo, she became a part of the bohemian literary crowd. In the years to follow, Chiyo often wrote about her lovers or husbands (she married three times). Her masterpiece, *Ohan*, was published in 1957. It tells the gentle story of renewed, but finally failed, love between a wife and the husband who had left her for another woman years before.

In the early 1970s, Uno and her third husband started Japan's first fashion magazine, *Sutairu* (Style),

and opened their own boutique, selling clothing she designed. In 1983 she published her best-selling memoirs and continued to write even when she was well into her 90s.

Alice Walker (1944–)

Novelist, poet, short-story writer, essayist

HAILED AS A FICTION WRITER, POET, ESSAYIST, AND lecturer, Alice Walker examines issues of racism and sexism through the struggles and survival of black women. She was born and raised in a large sharecropping family in rural Georgia, and she often makes use of memories from her childhood in crafting her writings.

An early accident with a BB gun left Walker blind in one eye and convinced that she was ugly. She retreated into reading and writing. Her hardship worked in her favor as well, though. Because of her disability, she received a scholarship to Spelman College, then transferred to Sarah Lawrence College. After graduating in 1965, she became an active participant in the Civil Rights movement and began working as a teacher. Her volume of poetry, *Once* (1968), was the first in a steady succession of published works. Although her writings were always acclaimed in academic circles, her Pulitzer Prize–winning novel, *The Color Purple* (1982), made her a nationally celebrated writer.

Alice Walker continues to use her writings to give voice to oppressed women worldwide. She has been criticized for devoting herself to feminism rather than to race issues and has responded by terming herself a "womanist," concerned with all womankind. Among her other books are the essay collection *In Search of Our Mothers' Gardens: Womanist Prose* (1983) and the novel *The Temple of My Familiar* (1989).

Wendy Wasserstein (1950–)

Playwright

WENDY WASSERSTEIN HAD AN INKLING OF HER future career when she volunteered to write the script for the mother-daughter fashion show at her high school so that she could get out of gym class. At Mount Holyoke College, she majored in history but devoted much of her time to theater. She went on to study playwriting at City College in New York, and her work, *Any Woman Can't*, was produced Off-Broadway in 1973. The positive reviews confirmed her career choice. Although she had been considering going to business school, she decided to study playwriting at Yale University instead. By 1977 she had produced her first hit, *Uncommon Women and Others*.

Wasserstein's plays usually center around the dilemmas of highly educated women much like herself. These women struggle with serious issues, but in hilariously comic ways. Other plays by Wasserstein include *The Heidi Chronicles*, which was produced in 1988, and *The Sisters Rosensweig* (1992). She has also written teleplays (plays written for television), film scripts, and humorous essays.

Simone Weil (1909–1943)

Philosopher, mystic, poet, political activist

Born in Paris to a wealthy Jewish family, Simone Weil demonstrated her brilliance at an early age. She was educated in the rigorous classical tradition and obtained a degree in philosophy from the École Normale Supérieure, the premiere teacher's education school in France. Afterward she taught philosophy at girls' schools. She also spent time performing various industrial and agricultural jobs. She later wrote about her experiences in *The Condition of the Workers* (1949). A pacifist, Weil supported the Spanish Republicans during the Spanish Civil War and joined the French Resistance during World War II.

To Weil the truth was not simple. She felt that it must be based on a synthesis of paradoxes. Deeply spiritual, she denied Judaism and, after a series of mystical experiences, expressed beliefs that were close to Catholicism. Her works remain controversial, but several are significant today, including *L'enracinement* (1949, published in English as *The Need for Roots*) and *Oppression et liberté* (1955, Oppression and liberty). She believed that "power transforms humanity into objects" and called for radical social change to create a better world.

Weil lived in London after the Nazis occupied Paris, growing increasingly despondent about world events. She died at age 34 from tuberculosis and self-imposed starvation—she had refused to eat more than the wartime rations she thought her countrymen could obtain.

Eudora Welty (1909–)

Novelist, short-story writer, photographer

Eudora Welty is one of the most celebrated voices in Southern fiction. Her favorite setting for stories is her home state of Mississippi, which she renders in lively detail and populates with complex characters. Her rich sense of humor and optimistic outlook pervade even her most serious stories.

Welty was born in Jackson, Mississippi, to progressive parents. In 1929 she received her bachelor's degree from the University of Wisconsin. She went on to the Columbia University Business School in New York, following the advice of her father, who wanted her to have a trade to fall back on if her writing career failed. By the time she graduated, however, the Depression had begun, and there were few jobs available. Welty returned to Jackson and began to write for local publications.

In 1933 she took a job photographing and interviewing Mississippi citizens for the Works Progress Administration, a government-sponsored program to provide employment for American artists during the Depression. Her observation skills served her well—her photographs have since received high praise from art critics—and the experience inspired her creatively. Welty was soon publishing stories in prestigious literary magazines, such as the *Sewanee Review* and the *New Yorker*. *The Curtain of Green and Other Stories* (1941) was the first of her many books. Her novel *The Optimist's Daughter* (1972) won the Pulitzer Prize, and her autobiographical work, *One Writer's Beginnings* (1984), was a best-seller. A private person, Welty still lives in Jackson.

"His memory could work like the slinging of a noose to catch a wild pony."

Eudora Welty
"First Love," 1943

Edith Wharton (1861–1937)

Novelist

As a girl, Edith Wharton was drawn to intellectual and artistic pursuits but caught in a world of superficial rituals. Her wealthy, conservative New York parents denied her formal schooling. The teenaged Wharton published poetry and a novel, but stopped writing after her parents rushed her debut into society. When she was 23, she married the proper Bostonian Edward Wharton, who was 35.

They were an ill-matched couple. Teddy had two interests—horses and dogs; his wife's brilliance intimidated him. He had no money of his own, and he squandered hers. The unhappy Wharton suffered a breakdown in her 30s, but the time she took to recuperate freed her to exercise her enormous creativity. She began writing novels, publishing her first great success, *The House of Mirth*, in 1905.

After divorcing her husband in 1913, Wharton lived mostly in Paris. She was known as a marvelous companion and conversationalist and welcomed many literary giants to her salon, most notably the novelist Henry James. In 1916 she was made a Knight of the Legion of Honor by the French Government for her refugee work during World War I.

Wharton wrote over 50 books, including *Ethan Frome* (1911) and *Summer* (1917). In 1921 *The Age of Innocence* was awarded a Pulitzer Prize. Using irony and precise detail, Wharton often wrote about the ways people of superior intellect and morality could be trapped by weaker characters.

Phillis Wheatley (1753?–1784)

Poet

When she was about eight, Phillis Wheatley was kidnapped by slave traders in West Africa and brought to America. There, she was sold to the Bostonian John Wheatley as a companion for his wife. Susanna Wheatley immediately saw that the girl was gifted and began to treat her like a family member. Phillis learned English, then Greek and Latin, too, becoming familiar with classics by Virgil, Horace, and Ovid. In a few years, she began writing poetry. In 1773 she went to London, where her book had been accepted for publication. *Poems on Various Subjects, Religious and Moral* (1773), is the first printed poetry book by an African American author. Later that year, she was given her freedom.

Wheatley's poetry shows that she supported the rebels in the American Revolution. She described events in the war and wrote the famous, "To His Excellency General Washington." Her most celebrated

poem, "On Imagination," with its lyrical description of artistic creativity, foreshadows the Romanticism of 19th-century poets.

After Wheatley married a freed slave named John Peters in 1778, her life descended into tragedy. Abandoned by Peters and living in poverty, she suffered the deaths of two infants and died while in childbirth for a third time. She was barely 30 years old.

Laura Ingalls Wilder (1867–1957)

Children's writer

LAURA INGALLS WILDER LIVED TO BE 90 YEARS old. Her first book, *Little House in the Big Woods* (1932), wasn't even written until she was in her 60s. Based on her own life on the frontier, Wilder's eight novels provide an honest portrayal. Her tone may be nostalgic sometimes, but she does not ignore family tensions, relations with Native Americans, or the harshness of pioneer life.

Wilder's own family wandered for years, stopping in Wisconsin, Missouri, Kansas, Minnesota, Iowa, and South Dakota, and barely scraping a living from the soil. Constantly working, she did farm chores, sewed shirts for 25 cents each, and taught school. Wilder and her husband, Almanzo, endured crop failures, fire, illness, and the death of two sons. Their daughter, Rose, survived to become a journalist. It was she who urged Wilder to put her thoughts on paper, helped her write, and made sure the books were published. In the 1970s and 1980s, a television show based on the *Little House* books attracted a devoted audience. The novels remain classics, beloved by readers of all ages.

Christa Wolf (1929–)

Novelist, short-story writer, essayist

CHRISTA WOLF WITNESSED MANY OF THE century's most dramatic political events. She was a girl in Germany during the Nazi regime and did not at first question Hitler's propaganda. As a young student, however, she began her lifelong support of socialism, choosing to live in East Germany. With the collapse of the Berlin Wall and the reunion of the country, the 60-year-old Wolf faced not just disillusionment at the fall of communism but criticism for having supported the East German government. Not surprisingly, political themes are central to her work. Her novels often portray women struggling with individualism, political ideals, and their role in society.

Wolf was born in Landsberg, then a German town, but today a part of Poland. Forced to leave when World War II began, the family settled in Mecklenburg. Wolf moved to East Berlin in 1953. In 1963 she published her first novel, *Der geteilte Himmel* (Divided heaven). Her subsequent novels include *Nachdenken über Christa T.* (1968, The quest for Christa T.) and the autobiographical work, *Kindheitsmuster* (1976, Patterns of childhood). Acclaimed in America as well as Germany, Wolf is also the author of essays and short stories.

Mary Wollstonecraft (1759–1797)

Writer, feminist

MARY WOLLSTONECRAFT WAS A BOLD REBEL, even for the revolutionary times she lived in. Her major work, *A Vindication of the Rights of Women* (1792), helped change the world by advocating equality and independence for women.

Mary Shelley (1797–1851)

The daughter born on Mary Wollstonecraft's deathbed was also named Mary, and she became a writer. In 1816 she and her future husband, the poet Percy Shelley, spent the summer in Geneva, Switzerland, where they often visited poet Lord Byron. One June night, a tumultuous storm trapped them at Byron's villa, along with his doctor, John Polidori. The group entertained themselves by reading ghost stories. Then Byron challenged each of them to write a haunted tale. Neither he nor Percy finished. Polidori wrote *The Vampyre.* Mary produced a chilling classic *Frankenstein* (1818)—about a monster created from corpses and given life by a power-hungry scientist.

Her beginnings were modest. At age 19 she left her abusive father's household in Yorkshire, England, to work as a lady's companion, a common job for well-born young women, which entailed accompanying and assisting a female employer while she traveled. Later, with a dear friend, Fanny Blood, she helped her sister, Eliza, leave a violent husband, and the three women opened a girls' school. Wollstonecraft wrote her first book, *Thoughts on the Education of Daughters* (1787), arguing for equal education for girls. But the school failed, so she reluctantly took a job as a governess.

Wollstonecraft found work with a liberal publisher in London. She joined in political discussions with the philosopher William Godwin, the radical Thomas Paine, and other supporters of the French Revolution. In 1792 she wrote *Vindication*, the first great example of feminist literature and still an influential document.

While living in Paris to experience the Revolution, Wollstonecraft fell in love with an American, Gilbert Imlay. They had a daughter, Fanny, but after Imlay abandoned her, Wollstonecraft attempted suicide. Returning to England, she resumed her friendship with William Godwin. They married in 1796. She died just a year later from complications during childbirth.

Virginia Woolf (1882–1941)

Novelist, essayist, critic

One of the 20th century's most innovative authors, Virginia Woolf used the flow of ideas, associations, and memories through her characters' minds to reveal the subjects of her novels. *Mrs. Dalloway* (1925) and *To the Lighthouse* (1927) are groundbreaking examples of this technique, known as "stream-of-consciousness" writing. She immortalized her deep friendship with Vita Sackville-West in the spoof biography, *Orlando* (1929), about a character who lives from the 1500s to the present, changing sex from age to age. The nonfiction works *A Room of One's Own* (1929) and *Three Guineas* (1938), in which she argues that a woman writer must have a place to work and an income, are important feminist texts.

Virginia Stephen was born into a cultured London family. Her father, Leslie Stephen, was a scholar. He educated Virginia and her sister, Vanessa, at home. She was 13 years old when her mother died

and she had the first of the severe mental breakdowns that tormented her all her life.

Writing brought Virginia fame and prestige. She became part of the Bloomsbury Group literary circle, one of whose members, Leonard Woolf, she married in 1912. Afterward she suffered another breakdown and attempted suicide. She wrote about her struggles with mental illness in an autobiographical essay, "Moments of Being," which was not published until 1976.

For 25 years, Virginia Woolf's creative life blossomed, and she was nurtured by Leonard. However, she suffered as World War II came to England. Hearing the aerial battles over her country house in Sussex, she filled her jacket pockets with stones and drowned herself in the River Ouse in March 1941.

Yosano Akiko (1878–1942)

Poet, feminist

Yosano Akiko published passionate and romantic poems in the early years of the century. Her work was subtly revolutionary: Women were traditionally forbidden to express emotion through writing, yet Yosano did so and became one of Japan's most acclaimed female poets.

Yosano was born and raised near Osaka. From an early age, she knew she would be a poet. When she was 18, she submitted her poetry to a magazine called *Myojo*. The poetry editor there, Yosano Tekkan, was so struck by the young poet's work that he helped her publish her first collection, *Midaregami* (Tangled hair) in 1901. The book made her famous. That year she moved to Tokyo and married Tekkan.

Yosano was also a literary critic and was a teacher—she founded a girls' school in 1921. Her husband died in 1935, and some of the most poignant poems in *Hakuishu* (1942, White cherry), published just after her own death, mourned his passing.

Marguerite Yourcenar (1903–1987)

Novelist, poet, historian, essayist

MARGUERITE DE CRAYENCOUR WAS BORN IN Brussels, Belgium. Her mother died when she was a few days old, so her father raised her alone. He taught her to read several languages and traveled with her. She wrote poems, and when she was 16, her father helped to devise her pseudonym—a near anagram of the family name—then published her work. She debuted as a novelist with *Alexis* (1929).

In 1939 Yourcenar visited her friend Grace Frick in the United States and decided to make it her home, adopting American citizenship in 1947 and living in Northeast Harbor, Maine. So it was a double honor when France inducted her into the Académie Française in 1980. She was given special dual citizenship because members must be French citizens, and she was the first female inductee.

Yourcenar often took years to write a book. Her most famous work is the historical novel *Les mémoires d'Hadrien* (1951, Hadrian's memoirs), an interpretation of the character of the Roman emperor as he neared death. Another masterpiece was *L'oeuvre au noir* (1968, later published in English as *The Abyss*), a novel set in Renaissance Europe. Her writings weave myth, history, and psychology into rich tapestries, dense with detail.

María de Zayas y Sotomayor (1590–1661/69?)

Novelist, scholar

NOT MUCH IS KNOWN ABOUT THE MYSTERIOUS María de Zayas y Sotomayor, one of the first Spanish women novelists. She was born in Madrid, and her father was a military captain. She was likely a member of a distinguished family, because her writings express a sophisticated and intellectual view of the aristocracy. It is not known whether she married, and there is no certain documentation of her life after 1647. Two death certificates exist, dated 1661 and 1669, for women named María de Zayas. Since that was a common name, it's possible that neither one was the writer.

Although poetry and a play by Zayas have survived, she is best known for her novellas, which she called *maravillas*—marvels. These are collected in two volumes, *Novelas amorosas y ejemplares* (1637, Exemplary tales of love) and *Desangaños amorosos* (1647, The disenchantments of love). Zayas explored the powerlessness of women in 17th-century Spanish society. Her passionate, despairing, and often gruesome tales center on female characters who suffer at the hands of their husbands or lovers. The stories were immensely popular even through the 18th century.

TIME LINE

By 3100 B.C.E.	In Egypt, hieroglyphic writing develops.
By 3000 B.C.E.	The Sumerians keep records on clay tablets, using a writing style that is called cuneiform.
Around 2300 B.C.E.	The first known writer, Sumerian priestess and poet Enheduanna, writes "Inanna Exalted."
By 1700 B.C.E.	The North Semitic alphabet develops in the lands along the eastern coast of the Mediterranean Sea. It is thought to be the source of all modern alphabets.
650 B.C.E.	Greek poet Sappho composes lyrical verses in praise of love and women.
6th century B.C.E.	The first books of the Old Testament are recorded.
1st century	The books of the New Testament are written down.
105	Although paper has existed in China for some time, the papermaking process is dramatically improved.
650	Caliph Othman organizes the Koran, the holy book of the Muslim religion that contains the teachings of the Prophet Muhammad.
991	Sei Shonagon joins the court of the Japanese Empress Sadako and keeps a diary of her experiences.
1010	In Japan, Lady Murasaki Shikibu writes *Genji monogatari* (The tale of Genji), the oldest known novel.
1032	The celebrated Chinese poet Li Ch'ing-chao arrives in Hungchao, China, after years of travel.
1041	Chinese inventor Pi Sheng makes a movable type printing press, but his idea will not catch on for centuries.
1163–1173	Hildegard of Bingen, a German mystic, poet, musician, and scientist, records her last book of visions, *The Divine Worship of a Simple Man*.
1406	The French writer Christine de Pisan is at the height of her popularity. She publishes *The Book of Three Virtues: A Collection of Moral Instructions*.
1434	In Germany, Johann Gutenberg experiments with ways to print books in large quantities. His movable type printing press makes books available to many more people.
1492	The explorer Christopher Columbus lands on San Salvador, an island in the Bahamas, and claims this New World for the Spanish King Ferdinand.
1630	Anne Bradstreet sets sail for the New World. She will become the first published poet in the English colonies.
1647	In Spain, Maria de Zayas y Sotomayor publishes her *Novelas y saraos* (Novels and soirees).

Aphra Behn

1688	Aphra Behn's *Oroonoko* is published. It is considered by many scholars to be the first English novel by a woman.
1700	Sister Juana Inés de la Cruz writes *Respuesta de la poetisa a la muy*

	illustre Sor Filotea de la Cruz (Reply of the poetess to the illustrious Sister Filotea de la Cruz), in which she expresses her desire for knowledge.
1726	The letters of Madame de Sévigné are published. Her insight, humor, and literary skill help to establish letter writing as an art form.
1773	Because no American publishers were interested in her work, Phillis Wheatley's first book appears in London. She is the first published African American poet.
1775–1783	The American Revolution. The Declaration of Independence is signed in July 1776.
1789–1799	Revolution in France
1792	Englishwoman Mary Wollstonecraft writes the first major piece of feminist literature, *A Vindication of the Rights of Women*.
1800	The Library of Congress is founded in Washington, D.C., to serve members of Congress. Over time it becomes the national library of the United States, housing one of the world's largest collections of books and documents, many of which are available to the public.
1810	Madame Germaine de Staël, a Swiss writer, publishes *De l'Allemagne* (On Germany), a satirical novel.
1811	In England, Jane Austen publishes her first novel, *Sense and Sensibility*.

19th-century novelist Jane Austen

1837	Harriet Martineau records her reflections on American society after touring the United States in *Society in America*.
1844	Margaret Fuller, an American feminist, publishes *Summer on the Lake* and opens the discussion of the displacement of American Indians.
1846	The English sisters Charlotte, Emily, and Anne Brontë publish their first book, a collection of poetry, under the pseudonyms Currer, Ellis, and Acton Bell.
1850	The first installment of Harriet Beecher Stowe's *Uncle Tom's Cabin* appears in the antislavery journal *The National Era*.
1861–1865	The Civil War in America
1862	Swedish feminist Camilla Collett publishes her memoirs, *I de lange Naetter* (During the long nights).
1868	The first volume of *Little Women: Or Meg, Jo, Beth, and Amy* by Louisa May Alcott is published.
1876	At the Philadelphia Centennial Exposition, the first typewriters are displayed by the Remington Company.
1886	*A White Heron and Other Stories* by the American regional novelist Sarah Orne Jewett is published.
1904	Japanese poet Yosano Akiko writes an antiwar poem entitled "Please Don't Die" as her brother goes off to war.
1906	Continuing her examination of classism in American society, Edith Wharton publishes the novel *The House of Mirth*.
1908	Canadian author L. M. Montgomery publishes her first novel, *Anne of Green Gables*. It proves to be wildly successful and inspires a whole series of *Anne* books.
1909	The National Association for the Advancement of Colored People (NAACP) is founded.

1914–1918 World War I

1915 American novelist and playwright Susan Glaspell cofounds the Provincetown Players with her husband and friends. Their first production is *Suppressed Desires,* written by Glaspell.

American writer Djuna Barnes publishes her first collection of poetry, *The Book of Repulsive Women.*

1916 An important and international year in poetry: Edith Sitwell, Amy Lowell, H.D., and Alfonsina Storni all publish collections of poetry.

1917 Revolution in Russia. During the time that follows, many intellectuals suffer persecution by the Communist government. The work of poet Anna Akhmatova is suppressed, but she refuses to leave her homeland.

Virginia and Leonard Woolf found the Hogarth Press. They will publish Virginia's work as well as the writings of other modernist writers such as T. S. Eliot.

Newspaper publisher Joseph Pulitzer leaves $50,000 to Columbia University for the establishment of annual prizes in journalism, letters, and music. Laura E. Richards and Maude Howe Elliott win the first biography prize for their book, *Julia Ward Howe.*

Dorothy Parker joins the staff of *Vanity Fair* magazine. Soon she and her writer friends begin meeting for lunch at New York City's Algonquin Hotel. Throughout the 1920s and 1930s, this group—the "Algonquin Round Table"—are legendary for their scathing and hilarious quips.

Humorist Dorothy Parker

1920 The 19th Amendment granting women's suffrage goes into effect on August 26th.

A time of great productivity and creativity—the Harlem Renaissance—begins as African Americans settle in New York City after World War I. It lasts through most of the 1920s.

1921 The first children's book award, the Newbery, is established by the American Library Association. The prize is named after John Newbery, who was an 18th-century bookseller.

1923 Willa Cather wins the Pulitzer Prize for her novel *One of Ours,* and Edna St. Vincent Millay becomes the first female winner of a Pulitzer Prize for poetry for her collective output.

1924 American writer Inez Irwin wins the O. Henry prize for her short story, "The Spring Flight."

1926 African American poet Gwendolyn Bennett serves as the editor for the short-lived periodical *Fire!!*

British mystery writer Agatha Christie disappears on the evening of December 3rd, and a nationwide manhunt begins. She is found in a hotel registered under a false name, and she claims not to remember how she got there.

1928 Miles Franklin publishes *Up the Country* about her native Australia using the pen name Brent of Bin Bin.

1929 "Black Thursday," the disastrous stock market crash of October 27th, signals the beginning of the Great Depression in the United States.

1935 Uno Chiyo, Japanese author and fashion editor, publishes her first acclaimed work, *Confessions of Love*, a novel about her artist lover.

1936–1939 The Spanish Civil War erupts between nationalist rebels and the weak republican government. Many American expatriate writers, artists, and intellectuals living in Europe are drawn to the cause. Among them is American Josephine Herbst.

1936 In Great Britain, Penguin Books issues inexpensive "paperback" editions of classic literature, a new and revolutionary marketing concept. Pocket Books brings the idea to the United States in 1939.

1938 Laura Ingalls Wilder wins a Newbery Honor for her young adults' novel *On the Banks of Plum Creek*. This is the first of her five recognitions by the Newbery committee.

1939–1945 World War II. Jewish poet Nelly Sachs flees Nazi Germany and settles in Stockholm, Sweden.

1941 American playwright Lillian Hellman receives the New York Drama Critic's Circle Award for her play *Watch on the Rhine*.

1944 In France Colette publishes her novella, *Gigi*. American writer Anita Loos adapts it into a play that is produced on Broadway in 1951. Seven years later, the play is set to music and made into a popular film.

1948 French writer and philosopher Simone de Beauvoir publishes the autobiographical work *Ethics and Ambiguity*, in which she discusses the philosophy of Existentialism.

1950 A group of organizations that are dedicated to book production—the American Book Publishers Council, the Book Manufacturers Institute, and the American Booksellers Association—establish the National Book Award to honor works by American authors.

1951 Chinese writer Ding Ling wins the Stalin Peace Prize for her novel *The Sun Shines on the Sangaan River*.

1953 Anne Frank's diary is published in America for the first time. A victim of World War II, the young Jewish writer had died eight years earlier in a German concentration camp. It quickly becomes a classic.

1959 The Cuban Revolution. Fidel Castro becomes the leader of the first Communist country in Latin America.

Sylvia Beach with writer James Joyce in Paris

Sylvia Beach publishes her memoirs, *Shakespeare and Company*.

1960 *The Complete Poems of Emily Dickinson* is published, almost 75 years after her death.

1962 American Anne Sexton publishes her second volume of poetry, *All My Pretty Ones*.

1963 German-born writer Hanna Arendt publishes *On Revolution*.

American feminist and author Betty Friedan achieves fame with her book *The Feminine Mystique*.

1964–1975 War in Vietnam. The United States enters the conflict as the ally of South Vietnam, battling Communist forces in the North.

1968 Booker plc (public limited company), a British-owned company dedicated primarily to food production, establishes the Booker Prize, to be awarded for the year's best novel.

1969 Elizabeth Bishop receives the National Book Award for *The Complete Poems*.

1970 American writer Grace Paley receives an award from the National Academy for Arts and Letters for short fiction.

1971 Maya Angelou publishes her first volume of poetry, *Just Give Me a Cool Drink of Water 'fore I Diiie*.

1972 British travel writer and explorer Freya Stark is honored with the title of Dame Commander.

1974 Leslie Marmon Silko publishes her first work, a collection of poetry entitled *Laguna Woman: Poems*.

South African writer Nadine Gordimer wins the British Booker Prize for her novel *The Conservationist*.

1975 Kay Boyle writes *The Underground Woman*, in protest of the Vietnam War; it is her last work.

1976 Ntozake Shange receives a Tony Award for her choreopoem, *for colored girls who have considered suicide/when the rainbow is enuf*.

1977 Three companies—Apple Computer, Radio Shack, and Commodore Business Machines—introduce their first personal computer models.

1979 Historian and writer Barbara Tuchman becomes the first woman president of the American Academy and Institute of Arts and Letters.

1980 Rita Dove publishes her first volume of poetry, *Yellow House on the Corner.*

Southern writer Eudora Welty publishes *The Collected Stories of Eudora Welty*.

1982 Isabel Allende, a Chilean writer forced into exile by a military takeover in her home country, publishes her first novel, *La casa de los espíritus* (The house of the spirits).

Nicaraguan writer Claribel Alegría publishes the book *Album Familiar* (Family Album, 1991).

1984 Louise Erdrich receives the National Critics Circle Award for her first novel, *Love Medicine*.

1986 German-born scholar Gerda Lerner publishes the first volume of her acclaimed work, *Women and History: Volume I, The Creation of Patriarchy*.

1987 Gore Vidal writes an essay for the *New York Times* calling for a revival of 20th-century writer Dawn Powell. Her work, which had been out of print, is revived.

1989 In Germany, the Berlin Wall is demolished following the collapse of the Communist powers in Eastern Europe.

American playwright Wendy Wasserstein is honored with a Pulitzer Prize, Drama Critic's Choice Award, and a Tony Award for her play, *The Heidi Chronicles*.

1990 German socialist Christa Wolf looks at the fall of Communism in her collection of essays, *Current Texts*.

1992 Susan Sontag, an American writer best known for her essays, publishes a novel, *The Volcano Lover*.

1993 African American novelist Toni Morrison receives the Nobel Prize for Literature.

1996 The annual Orange Prize for Fiction is established to honor the best novel published in Great Britain by a woman writer.

In October, television talk-show personality Oprah Winfrey announces that her show will begin a "Book Club." Within the year, Winfrey's endorsement is enough to make a book a best-seller.

GLOSSARY

Allegory: a story in which characters, objects, or events have a symbolic meaning beyond the superficial interpretation of the events described. Allegories are often intended to reveal universal or moral truths.

Anagram: a word or phrase that is made by rearranging the letters contained in another word or group of words.

Anthology: a collection of writings—usually poems, short stories, or essays—selected by an editor. The writings in an anthology may be by different writers or be chosen from different periods in a single writer's life.

Autobiography: the story of a person's life, written by that person.

Bohemian: originally, an inhabitant of Bohemia (now in the Czech Republic). Because this was an area where many gypsies settled, the word became associated with them and their unconventional lifestyle. Over time, it has come to apply to rebellious, free-spirited writers and artists.

Classical: in the literary sense, having to do with ancient Greek or Roman culture. When a person is "educated in the Classics," he or she is taught Greek and Latin languages and literature.

Existentialism: an influential, complex literary and philosophical movement that arose during the 20th century. The Existentialists argued that people are entirely free, and that they must determine their own fates by making choices, then taking action. They believed that no predetermined moral system (either religious or social) exists to govern or influence those choices, and therefore each person must decide how to proceed on his or her own.

Expatriate: a person who lives in a country other than his or her homeland, usually by choice rather than because he or she has been sent into exile.

Experimental: based on new ideas or techniques. Experimental writing or art usually involves the use of unconventional language, story construction, and imagery.

Exposé: a journalistic work in which corruption within a corporation or organization is revealed.

Free Verse: in poetry, lines that are irregular, do not conform to standard poetic rhythms, or meters. Usually free verse does not rhyme or contains subtle, hidden rhymes.

Gothic: a term used at first for the architecture that originated during the 12th century, when the Goths, a Germanic people, invaded Western Europe. Their stone buildings with ornamented arches and peaks were seen as wild, even barbaric. Much later, the idea was applied to a style of writing. The dark, eerie tales in "Gothick" novels deal with the supernatural, doomed love, and revenge.

Grotesque: from the old Italian meaning "from a cave" (or grotto). The word is associated with ancient Roman paintings that were excavated in the 16th century. At first, the fanciful, decorative images were thought to be cave paintings, but it was discovered that the sites where they were found were buildings. The word "grotesque" now describes an image or idea that is fantastic and bizarre.

Hymn: a religious song of praise.

Imagism: a movement in poetry during the 20th century. Practitioners strove to express themselves through clear, unambiguous images and often wrote in free verse.

Irony: a method of expression in which a word, phrase, or situation is intended to be interpreted differently from the literal words used or statement of the case. Sarcasm is a form of irony that is used negatively, to express scorn.

Lyrical: originally, a song intended to be sung to the accompaniment of a lyre. When used in a literary sense, "lyrical" describes writing, usually poetry, that has a musical rhythm and expresses profound emotion.

Manifesto: a declaration, usually written down, that makes public the artistic or political beliefs and intentions of a person or a group.

Melodrama: originally a theatrical work enacted in an exaggerated, sensational style. It has taken on a negative meaning in association with literary works that are too dependent on plot elements and wild actions at the expense of characterization or development of detail.

Memoir: writing that focuses on personal experience. Although it is autobiographical, the purpose of a memoir is to describe particular events or types of events, rather than the author's full life story.

Metaphor: a figure of speech in which a word or phrase associated with one context is used in place of a word or phrase to suggest a relationship between them. For example, "it's raining cats and dogs" draws a comparison between a torrential downpour and the image of animals falling willy-nilly from the sky.

Monologue: in drama or literature, an extended speech or section of the narrative that expresses the words or thoughts of a single character.

Mystical: having a spiritual meaning that cannot be understood through practical experience or logic and must therefore be revealed through intuition, contemplation, or religious revelation.

Novella: a fictional work that is shorter than a novel and longer than a short story.

Posthumous: occurring after a person's death. A book is said to have been published posthumously when it appears after its author has died.

Prolific: literally, "fruitful." It is often used to describe a writer or artist who has produced many works.

Prose: ordinary language, as opposed to poetry.

Pseudonym: literally, a "false name." The pen name (also popularly called by the French translation, *nom de plume*) chosen by a writer to mask or draw attention away from a real identity.

Salon: the French word for "drawing room" (roughly equivalent to today's living room), where guests were usually received. In literary and intellectual circles, a regular gathering for the purpose of discussing ideas is known as a salon.

Sardonic: skeptical and mocking.

Satire: a literary style in which humor and ridicule are used to expose human vice or foolishness.

Sonnet: a fixed poetic form that consists of 14 lines written in a five-beat rhythm (known as iambic pentameter) and rhyming according to set conventions.

Stream-of-consciousness: a style of writing in which events are presented as the flow of ideas, associations, and memories of one or more characters.

Tetralogy: a series of four related works (such as books or plays), each telling part of a longer story.

Theology: the study of religious beliefs and practices.

Whimsical: odd, fanciful, and unpredictable.

INDEX

Numbers in boldface type indicate main entries.

CREDITS

Quotes

10 Angelou, Maya. *I Know Why the Caged Bird Sings*. NY: Random House, 1979. Used by permission. **12** Austen, Jane. *Northanger Abbey*. London: Macmillan & Co., 1906. **16** Bradstreet, Anne. *The Works of Anne Bradstreet in Prose and Verse*. Charlestown: Abram E. Cutter, 1867. (Rendered in modern English.) **19** Burgos, Julia de. *Song of the Simple Truth: The Complete Poems*. Willimantic, CT: Curbstone Press, 1997. Used by permission. **22** Cleary, Beverly. From *Ramona the Pest*. Text © 1968 by B. Cleary. By permission of William Morrow and Company, Inc. **24** Dickinson, Emily. *Poems*. Boston: Roberts Bros, 1896. **27** Eliot, George. *Middlemarch*. NY: Doubleday, 1901. **34** Hellman, Lillian. *The Children's Hour*. NY: A. A. Knopf, 1941. By permission of Random House. **38** Julian of Norwich. *Revelations of Divine Human Love*. London: Methuen and Co., Ltd., 1911. **43** Li Ch'ing-chao. "Plum Blossoms Fall and Scatter." From Rexroth, Kenneth (translator). *One Hundred Poems from the Chinese*. NY: New Directions Books, 1959. Used by permission. **48** Moore, Marianne. "O to Be a Dragon" © 1957 by M. Moore, renewed 1985 by L. E. Brinn and L. Crane. From *The Complete Poems of Marianne Moore*. Used by permission of Viking Penguin, a division of Penguin Putnam, Inc. **57** Sévigné, Marie de. From Brockaway, W. and B. Winer (editors). *A Second Treasury of the World's Greatest Letters*. NY: Simon and Schuster, 1941. Used by permission. **61** Stein, Gertrude. *Tender Buttons*. NY: Claire Marie, 1914. **64** Tuchman, Barbara. Reprinted by permission of Russell & Volkening, agents for the author. Text © 1979 by B. Tuchman. Originally in *Authors League Bulletin*, Nov/Dec, 1979. **66** Welty, Eudora. From "First Love" in *The Wide Net and Other Stories* © 1942, renewed 1970 by E. Welty. Reprinted by permission of Harcourt Brace & Company.

Photographs

Abbreviations

AP	AP Wide World Photos	**HG**	Hulton Getty
COR	Corbis	**LOC**	Library of Congress

8 Adair, Virginia, photograph by Olivia Ellis. **9** Alcott, Louisa, LOC. **11** Arendt, Hannah, LOC; Aspasia, HG. **12** Barnes, Djuna, COR/Oscar White. **13** Beauvoir, Simone de, HG. **15 (and cover)** Blume, Judy, AP. **15** Bly, Nellie, LOC. **17** Brönte sisters, LOC; Brooks, Gwendolyn, Prints & Photographs Division, Schomburg Center for Research in Black Culture—The New York Public Library/Astor, Lenox and Tilden Foundation. **18** Browning, Elizabeth, Media Projects Archives; Buck, Pearl, HG. **20 (and title page)** Cather, Willa, LOC. **21** Christie, Agatha, HG. **22** Colette, HG. **23** Delaney, Shelagh, HG. **24** Didion, Joan, COR/Ted Streshinsky. **25** Doolittle, Hilda, LOC. **26 (and cover)** Dove, Rita, photograph by Fred Viebon. **27** Duras, Marguerite, HG. **28** Erdrich, Louise, photograph by Michael Dorris. **29** Ferber, Edna, COR/Bettmann. **31 (and 6)** Frank, Anne, HG. **32** Gilman, Charlotte, LOC. **33** Glaspell, Susan, LOC. **34 (and 7)** Hansberry, Lorraine, LOC. **35** Hildegard of Bingen, HG. **36 (and title page)** Hurston, Zora, LOC. **37** Jewett, Sarah Orne, LOC. **38** Juana Inés de la Cruz, LOC. **39 (and title page)** Lagerlöf, Selma, HG. **40 (and 7)** Lee, Harper, LOC. **42** Lessing, Doris, HG; Levertov, Denise, AP. **44** Loos, Anita, LOC; Lowell, Amy, by permission of Houghton Library, Harvard University. **46 (and 6)** Millay, Edna, LOC. **47** Mistral, Gabriela, LOC. **48** Morrison, Toni, photograph by TimothyGreenfield-Sanders. **49** Noailles, Anna de, LOC. **50** O'Brien, Edna, HG; O'Connor, Flannery, LOC. **52** Pisan, Christine de, COR/Gianni Dagli Orti. **53** Powell, Dawn, LOC. **54** Rich, Adrienne, LOC; Rossetti, Christina, HG. **56** Sappho, LOC. **57** Sexton, Anne, LOC. **59** Sitwell, Edith, HG; Sontag, Susan, Archive Photos. **60** Staël, Germaine de, LOC; Stark, Freya, HG. **62** Stowe, Harriet, LOC. **63** Tarbell, Ida, LOC. **65** Uno Chiyo, AP; Walker, Alice, photograph by Vachelle. **67 (and cover)** Wharton, Edith, LOC. **67** Wheatley, Phyllis, LOC. **69 (and cover)** Woolf, Virginia, LOC. **70 (and title page)** Yourcenar, Marguerite, HG. **71** Behn, Aphra, LOC. **72** Austen, Jane, Media Projects Archives. **73** Parker, Dorothy, LOC. **74** Beach, Sylvia, COR/Bettman.